NAN ÖSTMAN

Some Kind
of Company

Translated from the Swedish by Julia Rivers

Aspal Prime

Published in Great Britain in 2021 by Aspal Prime
an imprint of Aspal Press Limited
1 Quality Court, Chancery Lane, London WC2A 1HR

Originally published in Swedish in 1999 as 'Ett Slags Sällskap'

Copyright © Nan Inger Östman – licensed through ALIS Sweden

A catalogue record for this book is available from the British Library

ISBN 978-1-9162895-1-2

Printed in Great Britain by Book Printing UK, Peterborough

www.aspalpress.uk

Translator's Introduction

Nan Inger Östman (1923-2015) was a much-loved Swedish writer and for many years the most heavily borrowed author in Swedish libraries. In 1987 she won the prestigious Astrid Lindgren Memorial Award. Born and raised in Östermalm, a wealthy, tree-lined residential area of Stockholm she graduated from Stockholm University in 1946. Östman began her career as a journalist, firstly with the newspaper *Svenska Dagblad,* followed by a period at *Morgon Tidningen* where she stayed until 1955. She then worked as a teacher, initially at the prestigious Lundsberg boarding school. While teaching she began writing books and became a full-time author from 1980 onwards.

In *Some Kind of Company*, published in Sweden in 1999, Östman draws heavily on her own experience of Swedish life and society to give us a moving protrayal of Anna, a 72-year-old translator, living with her husband in the Swedish countryside. Her children have grown up and left home and her husband rarely speaks to her. She decides to bring about some much-needed change in her life by advertising for a male penfriend in a local newspaper. A correspondence ensues with a widower named Bo, which gives us some intriguing insights into the lives and characters of both Anna and Bo, and culminates in an outcome as surprising to the characters themselves as to the reader.

Penfriend?

72-year-old professional woman, a bit worse for wear, but healthy, hard-working, well-read, married, would like to exchange thoughts with single educated gentleman of mature years.

Reply to SvD 997 25 100

Answer to Bo Svensson

I never thought that I would receive so many answers to my advertisement – at seventy plus! (I believe that's how one describes one's age nowadays.) And married into the bargain. And at a time when most people prefer to use email and not many write ordinary letters. I read and pondered and felt a little saddened. Two of the letters were such heart-rending cries for help in their acute loneliness... but I am not a counsellor. I suspect that one reply was from a conman. He was, or claimed to be, fifty-two years old. What could he want with me, unless he thought that I had a bit of money saved up? There was something too ingratiating about the way he wrote.

For a whole day I worked on answering the letters, almost as if I were applying for a job and wanted to present the best possible image of myself. A sense of humour and tolerance are apparently of paramount importance in this sort of relationship. One might possibly agree with that – but are they really so essential?

This preamble shows how difficult it is to write to someone unknown. There's the risk of being misunderstood or misinterpreted. Perhaps I have overlooked a fundamentally warm and interesting person simply because they wrote too formally. I shall never know.

It seems you are the only remaining candidate because I can't imagine having two or three penfriends at the same time. There must be some order in life.

You wondered tactfully, and very kindly, what induced a probably well-brought-up lady to put an ad in the Personal column.

I too am wondering about that. It is so unlike my usual behaviour that I have surprised myself. I am a natural onlooker. I don't usually take the initiative and am afraid of being rejected. But I decided to do something unexpected, something just for myself, something that I hoped I would get a little kick out of. There is a lot I would like to talk about with a sensible person who doesn't know me and so has no preconceptions. It would be fun and exciting to start from the beginning again. Within limits of course.

I must make one thing clear straight away, even if it sounds foolish. I believe people can advertise for almost anything in Personal ads and others will reply. So, as the English say – *no sex please*. I think it sounds a bit less clumsy and a little more nonchalant in English. Though still silly. But it's best to say it straight out. There are men who are still virile well into old age (according to what I have read and heard) and I believe specialist erotica for old people is now available in books and films. Well, I am quite prudish and have nothing to offer a hungry old man in that respect.

So now I've got that off my chest! It wasn't easy.

You were wondering what I imagined my prospective penfriend would be like. It really doesn't matter, so long as you are kind. Well, reasonably kind at least and reasonably honest.

I would never forgive you if you laughed at my letters with a friend. And I certainly don't want a passionate pensioner. All I want is to exchange ideas in writing with someone who thinks a bit about life and people, although I am not myself profound or an intellectual. I don't think I will write any more about myself until I know if you still want to write to me after receiving this letter. There is also no hurry to reveal our true names and addresses. I would prefer to remain permanently anonymous.

You would obviously also prefer that too. Anyone who claims to be called Bo Svensson is presumably not too keen to reveal their true identity. And, yes, I did look in the phone book. There was no trace of a Bo Svensson at the address you gave.

You will obviously be wondering what is wrong with me, how I could have ended up in this situation. I am wondering the same about you.

Yours sincerely.

SvD 997 25 100

Dear Bo Svensson,

So you are an archivist. Or rather, were. It sounds learned, orderly and not particularly exciting. I can picture a round-shouldered man in a cardigan and white cotton gloves tiptoeing between shelves and filing cabinets in dark basements. But I suspect there is more to it than that.

I translate fiction and am pleased with every new commission I am given at my age. There are plenty of people ready and willing to snatch such jobs from the hands of an elderly person. If they succeed, I will not know how to fill my days.

I too grew up in Östermalm.[1] We probably met each other in the road on our way to school. We may also have met at high school – there were those school dances. After taking my Master's degree I ended up in book publishing. I am ashamed of how casually it happened thanks to Papa's connections. It tended to work like that in those days. I myself had high-flying plans to become a journalist, but you had to take the steady prospect rather than the less secure one – at least if you had a strong-willed mother like mine. And she was right. I would not have been a successful journalist. When Håkan (my husband) was appointed to a district court we moved from Stockholm. Then it was a matter of taking temporary positions in schools for a while. But I am not a natural teacher. I never in my life wanted to be one. Having a Master's in languages does not mean one is automatically suited to teaching them. I made my mind up to stick to books. I am simply a book person and without them would have experienced much less of life.

A translator is in some ways invisible, although one occasionally receives a small pat on the back from the critics. Naturally it is lonely work – no one to talk to, no one to take a cup of coffee with – and not at all glamorous. But archivists aren't exactly accustomed to being in the spotlight either, are they? Still, I like working with languages, twisting and turning words. As occupational therapy it is unsurpassed. I hope it will keep my brain going, though there's no guarantee. It might wear it out instead. Yesterday I saw the cutest little centenarian on TV. She had newly styled white hair, bright eyes and pink cheeks. She keeps herself going by playing bingo. I have never seen anyone more alert which would suggest that bingo is better for you than books.

I am very privileged not only in my work, but also my workspace. From the chair at my writing desk I can see our narrow road disappearing behind a hill with a towering savings bank oak tree[2] on top. If I lean a little to the right, I can see the church steeple sticking up over the fields like a newly sharpened pencil. The autumn-sown wheat is very green, and the newly ploughed fields shine with plump, wet loam. From the kitchen I have a view over the lake. Today it's overcast, with no wind, so the water is gray and dull, but the sycamores have begun to turn a rich shade of gold. I'm glad it's autumn. It soothes the soul.

Why not choose a female friend for myself, you were wondering. But, please – just think about it. I have female friends already. I don't want to write to one. For an older person who lives in the country and rarely sees other people, it is more stimulating to receive a letter from a gentleman.

Would you think it was so much fun to write to an unknown man?

If so, I think you should do it.

Otherwise, feel free to reply to me.

Yours sincerely

SvD 997 25 100

Dear Archivist,

So you think not. That's good.

Thank you for telling me about your work. I am ashamed of my earlier ignorant comments. Perhaps that was your intention? Now that I know a little more about it, I am horrified to think that you might put my letters in a folder and copy your own, and then have them all bound. I don't want to be immortalised! What I write should not be preserved and certainly should not be read by anyone other than you. And that is my answer to your question.

I don't really know what is meant by 'outer and inner style'. That mostly appears in Personal ads and perhaps also in obituaries. I don't have either of them.

No, I don't play golf. That probably belongs to the notion of outer style. In some circles at least. No, I don't do long-distance skating either, unfortunately. But sometimes I put on an old pair of tubular skates, which I have kept from my school days, and potter around on the lake. That's fun but I am not good at it. Every year I think that I should buy some long-distance skates, then I worry that I won't master the technique. And then snow falls on the ice and it's too late.

Yes, I like good food and in happy times am quite good at

cooking. And, yes, I like drinking. White wine in the summer, and otherwise red; or both if offered. In fact the latter has become more and more common over the years. It is as if it does not have as much effect on me as before, when a single glass seemed to enhance thought, word and deed. I am no connoisseur.

I have a feeling that I live slightly more casually than you do and am naturally more rackety; perhaps I take more for granted and think less than you do. In one respect, at least, you definitely have the advantage over me. As a widower you are no doubt distinctly sought after in certain situations. You have probably noticed that for yourself. There is a lot more I could say about this matter, but we will save that for another time.

Finally: you don't need to worry in the least about Håkan. Obviously, he does not know that I am even now sitting and writing to a complete stranger, but why should I tell him? He wouldn't be the slightest bit interested. He certainly doesn't open my post or read my letters.

You seem a bit bewildered by the fact that we live in the country but don't have a farm or any other rural landholding. There's nothing strange about that though. We rented a place in the country as a summer retreat when the children were small. It was intended to be somewhere the whole family, relations and friends could get together. Some years were almost exactly what we had expected. The sun shone, the children were happy and ran around half-naked with their playmates and cousins, while we grown-ups sat under the trees with friends on the warm summer evenings. Those were the times when no-one was ill, everyone was still alive and full of optimism.

Eventually we bought a house in the country and toiled away on repairs and renovations. But one needs time and money to make an old run-down house comfortable enough to live in. By the time we had achieved that, our children were much older, were attending language courses or going Interrailing. They wanted to work or earn money during the summer holidays. Eventually it was only at Christmas that we were all together in the country and it never became the family retreat for children and grandchildren we'd hoped it would be. For many years now it has been home to just Håken and me. But it's the only place I want to live in.

Obviously, we are very isolated. Almost in a vacuum.

We live a quiet life.

There's very little noise around here.

What is it like where you are?

Svd 997 25 100

P.S. Important. This is the last time you can send me an answer via the newspaper. They won't forward any letters from now on. I am racking my brains about how I can keep my anonymity. If we were children, we could put our letters in a hollow oak or behind a loose stone in a wall. But what do we do now? It is absurdly important to me to be anonymous. Just as it is for you, Bo Svensson. But's that not because I have anything to hide, something criminal or unbelievably shocking. I am completely ordinary.

Dear Old Archivist,

What a good idea – Poste Restante! From now on you must write to Anna Antonsson, Poste Restante, Bålsta. I don't have to prove who I am when I collect letters. I telephoned and enquired about it. I am really called Anna, so I have let go of a little of the secrecy.

As for your worries – the fact that no grandchild's birthday would have been forgotten when your wife was alive, far less your daughter's... Well, of course not! Mothers and grandmothers know instinctively when a birthday is approaching and always arrange something nice. Fathers and grandfathers, on the other hand, have to have all important dates written down for them and must constantly check them. It is a typical gender difference and nothing to worry about. Although you are an archivist and particular, you can't help forgetting such things.

You must understand that women like to look after everything and to be the ones who keep order in the family. We are also experts at keeping men out and appoint ourselves as the contact between children and parents. Then we sit there full of children's confidences and select which bits of news to hand on, while fathers feel passed over.

13

You write that you are having a hard time coping with the emptiness after a long marriage. It doesn't even help to spend time with friends or do research (which you modestly call your little hobby). But isn't that only natural?

One must be realistic. There are few people who have everything at our age. Many struggle with ill health, financial problems, difficult children, quarrelsome wives or husbands. Not many are completely healthy, clear in the head and have a partner. We age in one way or another all the time. It's sad but inevitable. And you must have had a very good marriage, if you are feeling so much grief.

While we are on the subject of sad things: yesterday I cleared out a box of old letters and diaries. I burned most of them, so that the children would not have to be ashamed of me should they happen to read them once we are gone. I felt some pain on seeing them burn. This morning I carried out the ashes and put them around the currant bushes – fertilising them with my youthful despair and gloomy thoughts on betrayal and love. There will probably be large black berries as a result in the summer. Everything serves a purpose.

Speaking of parents and children: did you accept their becoming independent with good humour and understanding? We certainly didn't manage it. But I guess being brought up by parents whose own parents had been born in around 1870, and in their turn had been raised according to Lutheran teaching, left its mark on us all. I regret a lot when it comes to my daughter Malin. Lasse got off more lightly.

As for the rest – took a long walk, found chanterelles. Yellow leaves, low sun, eager dog running off in search of a scatter-brained hare. Came home happy and in a good mood.

Otherwise pleasures are few and far between. There was a

time when we went to the theatre and cinema regularly. Now we seem to have lost the will. It's so dark outside and a long way to Stockholm.

Take care of yourself.

Anna

PS. Who is Ellen?

Dearest Archivist,

I smiled when I read that your wife was constantly wandering around at night to ensure that respectability was maintained when boys were hanging around your house. She still claimed to be broad-minded just like me, but naturally that didn't apply to her own children. And you refused to play policeman, just like Håkan. Men have nothing against their women making themselves look ridiculous so long as they are let off.

But we were desperate! I believed in all seriousness that I really saved Malin from a degenerate life. I actually imagined that it was dangerous for girls to begin having sex too early. Now I know better. Those girls I then thought were little trollops have become solid citizens with well-behaved children and responsible jobs. It would have been better if I had allowed Malin more freedom.

It was different with Lasse. I was certainly afraid that he might fall into the hands of someone really nasty. He was clueless! I didn't understand how all that was even possible with Malin for a sister but I suppose he knew more than we realised – otherwise there would have been no Carina.

I wonder if we were the last generation to be shy with our

children and afraid to intrude on their lives. We assumed that they were sophisticated but worried about them at the same time. Above all we wanted everything to go well for them in life, that they should work hard at school and obviously go further in their studies. We wanted to be proud of them. My goodness, what demands we made on them, poor things! It occurs to me that those 'bourgeois values' which one so often sees mentioned in the Personal ads might be about that. But of course, it's more about politics, money and career.

I often think about the lines of Harriet Löwenhjelm.[3]

> *Oh God! What is still so sad*
> *Is that nothing will ever happen,*
> *That our lives have become so bourgeois*
> *And we feed our souls with dross*

I don't live a proper life. It is deficient in every possible way. My inner person isn't flourishing. My outer person goes around in baggy checked trousers. I am still enough of a townie that I think we should wear out our clothes in the country, where one isn't seen. We have never understood what casual clothes are, Håken and I. But don't for one moment think that we live in poverty. We still have something to put on our bread and family heirlooms in our house.

And I am still alive. It could be worse. But I have to accept that the familial tie which for a long time went from heart to heart has been stretched out so far by this situation that the elastic could break at any time. Such a thing happens when children live in a foreign country.

Now I have become a bit pathetic so I will finish here.

Anna

Dear Archivist,

You have only yourself to blame, asking to hear more about the children as you did. If I begin it will be like turning on the tap of a barrel. Everything will just flood out. Malin is the eldest. After having had a turbulent youth she is now 'a career woman'. She is nearing forty, good looking, with a degree in law and economics, *singel* (that's what it's called nowadays) and with an enormous circle of friends. She is living in Brussels among others devoted to their careers. She has really outgrown her parents and all that we represent. But I only allow myself to be impressed to a limited extent because I know her weaknesses. We are proud of her but also a little disappointed. Sometimes I wish that she would come home to Sweden, get married to a nice man and have some children. It's urgent. Time is not on her side. So you see how petty-bourgeois I am – as if a husband and children meant happiness. But life is poor without children.

Lasse is another matter; more like other people, but perhaps a bit better behaved. Nowhere near as ambitious as his sister. He did well at the Technical College and has a good job. His partner is called Carina and she is a physiotherapist, stubborn, and always knows best. They live in Värmland and our grandson is called Simon and is four years old. Carina has a daughter called Emma who is one year older and a thousand times smarter.

A while ago Malin and Lasse came on a visit together to check up on us. They came to see how old we had grown and if we still seemed to be managing on our own. It was as though they had trouble accepting that we had a right to be old. When we go on our customary dog walk with them, they set a very fast pace. But we have our pride and keep up – despite the pain in our joints afterwards. Our children have no experience of older people. They scarcely remember their maternal grandmother and the rest of that generation had died already before Håkan and I were married. I don't think they are usually worried about us, but sometimes they suddenly seem to be. I can't remember if I was worried about my mother when I was their age – and she was frail, which can't be said of us. Young people are meant to be preoccupied with themselves and their own affairs. So why should Malin and Lasse think about us if not for the fact that there is a small peculiarity about us and our long marriage... Actually I hadn't planned on revealing that to you but obviously it's significant so I'd better.

You see, Håkan does not speak to me. And he only speaks a very little with everyone else. He gradually stopped talking. There is nothing wrong with him that prevents him from speaking. He can when he wants to and when it's essential. But I doubt whether the children really know how quiet it is here on weekdays. Although perhaps it is not so unusual that old people stop speaking to one another. And not listening to each other is normal if anything. Probably.

We live in a remote place so the silence isn't so noticeable. In the country it is not unusual for many people to be strange in one way or another. And there are many things that are worse than being silent. It's nothing to beat yourself up over. People have got used to it. We have been living here for a long time.

You shouldn't think that we live in a bitter silence because it isn't like that. At the beginning it was probably a way of punishing me. Through silence Håkan could shield himself from anyone who annoyed him and obviously I sometimes belonged to that group. I like talking – but not without ever being interrupted.

We are not one of those old couples who are spiteful to one another. Old people can sometimes be really mean but still stay together. Marriage is certainly strange. You use each other in different ways and for different purposes. I have been the most useful one. Perhaps.

Even someone who doesn't speak is some sort of company. Silence doesn't make such a difference because when it comes down to it, we don't have so much to say to each other. The radio and television talk to us, even if Håkan is no longer particularly interested in what they have to say.

Perhaps to me he's like the towel rail in the shower room. Every morning I do my exercises in there. I stand on one leg and bend up the other so that I can grasp my foot with my hand and pull the sole of my foot towards my back. Usually I keep my balance – one has to count up to thirty while standing like that – but sometimes I am unsteady. Then it's good to be able to hold onto the rail.

Do you know what the exercise is good for? The thigh muscles. Try it if you don't believe me.

Now you have got a monster of a letter. But I warned you. And I still don't know who Ellen is.

Anna

Dear Archivist,

You seem to be more interested in Håkan than in me! And it feels as though you are taking his part. That is understandable. It is hardly a recommendation of me that I have driven my husband to silence. That is what you think, isn't it, even if you don't say it out loud?

The fact is that I don't discuss Håkan with unknown people and barely with those I do know. We shall see later if it is possible for you to qualify as being someone who can be confided in. First you have to actually make some effort.

You yourself haven't exactly overwhelmed me with information about your wife. I have the feeling that she is viewed as almost 'holy' and that you definitely want to keep her out of our correspondence. The dead are very good at taking control. As are the silent. Is that why you seem to empathise with Håkan as an ally? But you should know that he is no hen-pecked husband. Quite the opposite. Remember that those who say nothing don't expose themselves, and in that way they always manage to have the last word. You can't argue with a person who is silent.

Thank you for telling me about Ellen. I understand that anyone of our age who still has an aunt alive must take great care of her.

I am in a bad mood (which is probably obvious), have finished my translation and have nothing new to start working on. Outside a keen east wind is blowing. The leaves swirl on the ground, the wind whistles in the chimney and there is a draught around our feet in this poor old house. I am always upset by the wind. Anyway, it isn't just windy. There is a storm blowing and the lake is slate-coloured and scattered with white caps. It helps to bake bread, if you want to feel peaceful. So that is what I will do. And then read Hjalmar Söderberg.[4] Although sometimes I would like to shake his characters to make them understand that one *can* change one's life.

Your grouchy Anna

Good Archivist,

Sorry, sorry, sorry! I was thoughtless and stupid, but how was I to know that your wife bore her cancer with such courage and with such consideration for you all at the end? I do not know what I should say to you. It is hard enough to know what to say to good friends when they are struck by the hand of fate. And I barely know you.

I was clumsy, I know that. And you think that in any case I should consider myself lucky not to be LONELY. What do you know about that?

But we shouldn't get into a competition about who has it worse. That wouldn't be good for either of us. Look, I don't understand you any longer. You who have been so reserved and a real example of 'inner style' suddenly showered me with bitterness.

I imagined that you saw life through more friendly eyes than I do, and sometimes from a different angle. That was exciting. Now it seems that I hear a familiar old song again, tinged with a bitterness that is different from what I am accustomed to hearing from you. When it comes down to it, it seems that you are a Disappointed Old Man who feels that he has been cheated by life.

I have listened to a lot of worried people. I have done my limited best but I will not be used as a wailing wall on which a man may vent his outrage and resentment once again. My stock of sympathy and encouragement is exhausted. It is just as well for you to realise now: no one is coming to your rescue. You have to wrestle with your own problems. Children can't help – they can barely manage to cheer us up. They have their own concerns and those are more important to them than our problems.

I have been wondering if you think it is time for us to say thank you and goodbye to each other? It was nice while it lasted. And it was very good that we kept to the strict anonymity plan.

With all best wishes

Anna

P.S. It just occurred to me – how do you manage to keep fit? Do you take vitamins and minerals? Or perhaps you aren't entirely healthy?

Dear Bo,

So you want to continue in spite of everything. It is almost pitiful that we two expect so little from life. But I am happy to go to the post office and collect a letter again.

You insist that you are as fit as a fiddle – in an injured tone! That's exactly what I thought. Cross-country skiers must be fighting fit and weather-beaten. Sometimes I see all the world going by on the lake below my window. They have ice prods slung round their necks and carry huge rucksacks. They really fly past while I feel like a tame goose who wants to take off and follow them but is too timid and too heavy.

Anyway, there isn't any ice yet. But I don't have to accept that I am slow and fixed in my ways. I am trying to conjure up for you a picture of me at the head of a group of walkers with an ice pick in my hand, white hair under a knitted hat, tall as a Viking, with piercing blue seaman's eyes and slightly downy ears, which are kept all the time alert for the sounds coming from the ice. Does that picture seem as unlikely as that of a round-shouldered man in a grey cardigan among the shelves?

Today I have been tidying up because tomorrow a pair of elderly childhood friends are coming for a visit. Can you

25

understand why so much of our short time on this earth is taken up with cleaning the summer's fly mess from windows and ledges? And why do we imagine that guests will be thinking about our standards of cleanliness? That is not why they visit. I believe they come out of the goodness of their hearts. They say to themselves, 'We must see something of the old couple before they go to pieces completely.' And they think about how much fun we had together once, even though it was a long time ago.

This letter has been lying about. I didn't get round to posting it. But the visit went well, almost as if Håkan and I were completely normal. Our friends like him. I could see that from the way they constantly tried to draw him into conversation. Anyway, we laughed a lot and looked at our present existence rather gloomily, since nothing seems to improve with the advancing years.

Then they went and it was as if a blind had been pulled down. Håkan withdrew into himself and nothing more was heard from him. Not a word was said. Not a single comment. It was as if our visitors had never been.

Anna

Dear Bo,

So the picture of a weather-beaten Viking in steel-toed boots didn't work. Pity. I was so pleased with it.

By the way, I still haven't heard from the publishers. This has never happened to me before; not being offered a new job as soon as I finished the last one. I hardly dare to be out of hearing distance of the telephone in case they should ring. I get so depressed when nothing happens. It feels as if I have been spurned and rejected. It hurts almost as much as it did when I was young and over-sensitive.

I am restless and find it difficult to make the time pass. The house is so clean that even the spiders have disappeared. It feels as though life is running through my fingers when I sit in the middle of the afternoon with a book in my hands and should enjoy being free.

I love working. I can't cope with being idle. I am reduced to tapping my teeth from sheer boredom and succumb to all kinds of little ailments, if I can get away with it. People who are newly pensioned off die like flies when they are deprived of work, and people say, oh, so sadly. 'And he was so happy to be free!' Good heavens, he was not! He was only pretending. I can swear to that. Have you too suffered from pensioner's anxiety? Is that why you have so much structure to your days? Anyway, I will never join a pensioners' club with coffee and dancing on the agenda. Why on earth should one dance during the day just because one is a pensioner, when one has never done so before. I don't think it makes sense.

Nor do I want to play bridge even if I could learn how to. That can't be the point of life – to spend your last days playing cards.

Write something uplifting to me.

Anna

Dear Bo,

I was in Stockholm the other day, entirely legitimately as my optician is there. I have lots of aches and pains but nothing that I can't recover from. The consulting rooms are close to St. John's Church and since I was there anyway I went and stood in the garden and wondered in which house Lydia[5] lived. Obviously I also read the inscription on Döbeln's[6] gravestone: 'Honour-Duty-Will'. I thought to myself, as I often do, that life must have been more manageable in earlier times when one could fortify oneself with a real mouthful of big words.

When I went to school we had to learn a lot by heart until we knew a text perfectly – speeches such as: "Men at some time are masters of their fates: The fault, dear Brutus, is not in our stars, but in ourselves, that we are underlings." 'Girls,' said the teacher, looking at us with piercing eyes, 'never forget those words!' And I never dared to, not a word, semicolon or comma was lost, and now and then, when I am in a crisis I still repeat those lines to myself like some kind of spell. Not that it has ever really helped, but it strengthens the backbone a little. How do you think young people fortify themselves nowadays?

Be that as it may, I went through the churchyard and thought of Arvid Stjärnblom [7] and his son. The one he had with 'that little shopgirl.' Then I thought of the child of Thomas Weber and Märta Brehm,[8] and of Söderberg's own children. It all sounds so absolutely dreadful. The children dragged hither and thither, taken from one place and sent to another without ever being asked what they wanted. It was as if their feelings were completely irrelevant. And what became of the 'literary' children? That wasn't of the least interest to the writers as far as anyone knows. They are pale, thin creatures; eternally lost souls who are only named in sub-clauses. It is difficult to get them out of one's mind. Then I went up to S. John's Church – it looked beautiful with a cold turquoise sky behind the church tower – and lamented the way that unwanted children were treated at the turn of the century. Then it occurred to me that things haven't really improved so much during the last hundred years. Even for those who are wanted. I think about Emma – the daughter of my son's partner. One week she lives with her natural father and his new family and the next with her mother and Lasse. And that's how it goes. Backwards and forwards, hither and thither, while her half siblings can stay where they are. Can one feel safe and loved in that situation? Or is it perhaps some compensation that one has two bedrooms, two bicycles, two sets of toys, two bookshelves?

Perhaps after all it wasn't so heartless to place a child with an 'honest working-class family' until they saw which way things were going. All parents want the best for their children. But still it often goes so wrong. It must be wonderful to have had a reasonably happy childhood. Did you?

Anna

Dear Bo,

Oh dear! I really put my foot in it again! But how could I have known that you had been a foster child? In my ignorance of the real world I thought that it mostly happened in books – for example, those of Harry Martinson[9] and Tora Dahl.[10] Believe me, I wasn't trying to be funny. But now I am curious and would like to know more. What was it like to be suddenly 'acknowledged' after having been a foster child with an 'honest working-class family' in Älvsjö, to be taken home in triumph and suddenly acquire three unmarried sisters for a mother?

But I suppose I must let you preserve your childhood memories in peace. (If you really don't want to talk about it.) You are right to say that far too many people complain about their unhappy childhood well into old age and blame it for everything that went wrong for them afterwards.

For quite a while I thought that anonymity was a kind of protection. Well, almost. But what kind of a dark impulse is it that makes someone want to talk about their thoughts and experiences to an unknown person? A stranger on the train for example. Is it so important to be heard, even when one doesn't know the person who is listening? I take it for granted that you are

Name: Nan Östman

nice and harmless. That's the impression I have from your letters. But I am useless at assessing people. For all I know you could be a bit mad. I imagine you sitting there with my letter in your hand and sneering at it with ice-cold eyes!

There is something weird about this way of socialising, that's for sure.

Anna

Dear Bo,

You have almost convinced me that you are not a madman, but until we meet in person .... You're right, though, we'd have to do it without taking any unnecessary risks. Even if you are mad, that's fine. We could just not write anymore if we take against each other at first glance.

But let's leave it there for the moment and move on – you correctly observe that it now seems to be our civic duty to keep fit and not to lay the burden of our ill health on society. If we just walk, do gymnastics, weight-lifting, and eat healthily, we're told we will feel good. But that isn't correct. Håkan's body is healthy to the core, but his soul huddles gloomily in its healthy prison.

Fourteen days ago, when I was visiting Stockholm, there were only pensioners visible, particularly in Östermalm. They were remarkably slim and elegant, all seemed healthy and fit. They had the sheen of wealth; looked as though they felt they had every right to maintain themselves in this privileged style. Everywhere I glanced, there they were – vigorous, cultivated, and well-travelled; with or without a dog; with or without a cane; with or without a partner. Completely irrepressible.

If all goes as expected, perhaps I too will come to look like that. My sister does and several of her old classmates. But I have 'fallen out of the top drawer'. I think I am classless.

Would you be at home in such a group? If the answer is yes, then I must tell you that I am the wrong person for you. It's not that I don't like those people but I don't fit the mould. My views are different and I never wear the right clothes for the occasion. And those blandly happy people frighten me a bit. One imagines that they don't have a dark side to their lives, nothing that couldn't bear the full light of day.

I no longer know where I belong: in some sort of grey area between classes probably. My trajectory today is downwards – and not upwards as it is for those who call themselves socially mobile. Those of us who are going slowly downhill talk less about the journey.

Perhaps you are right after all. Perhaps we should meet. We don't have that much time left.

We must certainly think about it.

Anna

The photo he was looking for must be in one of the earlier albums. They had sometimes talked about having it enlarged and putting it in a frame. Obviously Louise was not looking her best. It had been taken before the operation. Her left eye was squinting uncontrollably. A pity to have exactly that photo on view. They hadn't given it much thought. But that was who Louise was.

Anyway, here was what he was looking for. July 1967. At Rådmansö. The best photo he had ever taken of Marianne. She was laughing at him, just as he remembered her – healthy even teeth, clearly defined cheekbones, hair bleached by the sun, her collarbones sharp under her bathing-costume's shoulder straps. She was very sweet, his Marianne. He looked at the picture for a long time. Say what you like but she'd had style. And when the children were young, had wielded absolute control over the whole family. Splendid Ulrika on her knee, squinting Louise leaning on one side and a flaxen-haired Karin, with a plaster on her knee, on the other.

They had been happy years. Everything was good. Louise's eye problem was only temporary. It would be all right. And it was. But there was still something wrong with her. She saw things in a different way from her sisters. Perhaps she had had a distorted view of life from the beginning. Not even Marianne had been able to put that right.

But those were happy years. He turned the pages of the album. The girls among sandcastles, on the swings, in the water, on tricycles, on bicycles, and in boats wearing huge life jackets. The lion's share of pictures were of Karin, the eldest, with fewer of Louise and of Ulrika fewest of all. The urge to take photographs diminished over years of repetition. He could almost hear Marianne. 'Look, Bosse![11] Hurry up and fetch the camera!'

Had she already begun to bully him or did he of his own accord fetch the camera or whatever else – swimming floats, bathing wraps, balls? She had been so strong, his Marianne, and under that frivolous, girlish exterior concealed a will of iron. Things happened as she wanted them to. And it almost always turned out well. She wasn't just strong-willed. She was also clever, and good in an unsentimental way.

Life felt very empty without her. The loss was now a part of him. It was woven into his very fabric. It didn't help as much as he'd expected that he had children and grandchildren whom he often met. The children had never taken first place in his life. Days could pass without his thinking of them, or maybe only fleetingly. Marianne would have been displeased with him for that. She had photos of them all on a particular shelf by her bedside and she never lay down without giving each and every one of them a light caress with the tips of her fingers.

After the move the photos were placed on the book-shelf in his bedroom. But he seldom looked at them. And there was certainly no question of giving them goodnight kisses with his fingertips.

But the flood of news about the family had undeniably dwindled since Marianne no longer sat on the telephone almost every evening and checked on what was happening. She had censored the news. Anna had been right about that. He heard only what she thought would interest or amuse him, though the more negative news did gradually creep out. Louise had never done well in examinations, could never find work and seemed determined to stick to poorly paid jobs. She had no structure to her life at all. One year it was Jan, the next Conny and sometimes she appeared with men no one had seen before and who never seemed to have any social background, just a first name. No children obviously but had there been abortions? He didn't know and didn't want to know.

He didn't think that any of his daughters had led a particularly easy life. Capable Ulrika with her two children with eczema and a husband who was neither helpful nor happy. Karin who worked full-time, had three children, a man with a good career and also a pony for Sofia. A pony who mostly stood still and racked up expenses. Bo became a little angry every time he thought of that pony. It was only a status symbol, as anyone could see that Sofia would never make a rider. Even he, the child's grandfather, could see that, and he was no expert on horses. But Marianne, ambitious as always, had had great expectations of her granddaughter winning cups and rosettes. Even when she was at her most sick she asked after the pony. It was particularly strange in view of the fact that she had never previously been interested in animals. Perhaps the wretched pony stood for something she'd missed in her own life. Obviously she was very pleased about it and believed that it would be good for Sofia. He didn't know how she reasoned. He was able to understand her concern for their three daughters but did not really share it. They had to make their own choices and lead their own lives. They had grown up now. But she could never accept that.

It was a bit like no longer being the captain of the ship. But what she had found most difficult to reconcile herself to was that her role in their upbringing hadn't had any lasting effect on them – except possibly on Ulrika who had inherited her inflexible sense of duty. Truly her mother's daughter.

Perhaps it would have been better if there had been just a little indifference on her part instead of so much love. But no one could have claimed that Marianne burdened her girls with her attentions. Instead she determinedly invested all her spare reserves of energy in her teaching role at a school. As form-teacher she never gave up on a single pupil in her class. She stood by them through thick and thin. Not even the dullest of them was ever considered a lost cause.

It was a puzzle to him how the sweet, happy, slightly untidy little girl, that he had once fallen in love with, could have developed into such a formidable teacher. '*Du styrde, du ställde, du ville så väl …*'[12] He could not see those banal lines in an obituary without thinking of Marianne, when she was at her sickest. But she was quite aware of her own tendency to over-achieve. 'It's fortunate that I have a sense of humour,' she often said, 'otherwise I would be intolerable.'

Although he loved her, he had to admit that was true. It was lucky that she'd had a sense of humour, just a pity that she'd needed to talk about it so often. It was as if that gift had been bestowed upon her to enable her to put up with any difficulty – him included. She had never loved him as much as he had loved her. He couldn't expect that.

He looked at the young laughing mother in the photo and

wondered, as he so often had before, whether it had been his fault that she became so domineering. But they had got on well together despite it and when the girls left home it was even better. They'd had more time for friends and enjoying themselves, even if her work encroached upon their private life. Nervous schoolchildren waited in the hall to speak to her and tearful teenage voices asked for Marianne on the telephone almost every hour of the day. He never got used to the fact that she was no longer 'Mrs Rydeman'. He considered it disrespectful like so much else at that school.

And then she became sick and died, barely six months after she retired. Against all expectations. Statistically speaking, it was he who should have died first. He was a man, he was four years older than her and he had been delicate as a boy. Marianne had never been delicate, not even for a minute of her life. He was definitely physically weaker, inclined to stomach pains and headaches. A bit of a hypochondriac to put it bluntly. She despised mollycoddling of any kind. You had to have a really high temperature in order to be taken seriously. But then she really went into action. The only demand she made was that one should get better quickly. Illness should not become a habit.

And then she was the one who fell sick.

It was completely unexpected and developed so quickly. It was terrible. He tried not to think about it anymore. Just as he had expected, she managed better than he did. Even if she died in the attempt. Bald, thin, beautiful and stubborn to the last, she organised the rest of his life for him. He himself expressed no views about it.

'It's lucky that I can laugh at my own meddlesomeness,' she often said in those days. He mostly sat and nodded his agreement, notepad at the ready. She dictated and he wrote it down. She dealt with all the practical problems from the hymns to be sung at the funeral to the reception afterwards. The school choir should sing and the hymns should be chosen more to suit the choir's ability than her own wishes. Later it turned out that she had made all the right decisions. In that as in every other thing.

There were no objections to what she suggested. She did everything with all her might. And she knew better than he did what he would need and what he would find difficult to manage. And in any case, she suspected that he would not follow her advice in its entirety when he was alone. True, he was sitting there like a bird with its wings clipped then, but when it came to it he could take off. 'Just think about it,' she said, 'widowers are attractive to women. Don't let yourself be taken in by flattery. And whatever you do, don't get married again! That would cause problems with the girls.'

He could almost feel her presence behind him when he sat looking at the album. It was as if she were peering over his shoulder to get a better view of the photos of the children and herself. For a moment she felt so near that his right hand opened at the muscle memory of feeling the thick short grey down on her bald head. He had stroked it so many times during those difficult days. It felt like stroking a cat the wrong way.

We had a good time together; she would say in her unsentimental way. But no one would want you to live on memories for the rest of your life. Least of all me. You like women and you need someone to hold hands with. Take a look at that damaged letter writer, not that she seems to be right for you, but all the same… You are not so good at getting by on your own, not for long anyway. Think carefully about it and don't get involved in something you can't get out of. Remember that I can no longer help you. And if – against all expectations – something comes of it, you have my full blessing. 'Good luck,' she would have said then, just as she had when Louise went off to an examination. One of those eternal exams with unfair questions on the notes inserted in small type right at the bottom of some soiled page in a textbook. Poor Louise, predestined for misfortune. Just like her father, now that Marianne was no longer there to look after him.

Slowly he put the album away. He hadn't anyway yet decided whether or not to go to the meeting place. He had not even got used to her name yet. Anna. That was a name he had respected when he was a child. His first teacher in the elementary school had been called Anna and she hadn't been someone to trifle with.

Why had he suggested NK[13] as a suitable rendezvous point? True, the meeting was at his suggestion, but he was not obliged to go through with it. It could be embarrassing. He didn't need that. She mustn't get her hooks into him.

He was a free man and could do whatever he wanted. And he had decided that he didn't want a strange person in his life. Least of all someone with a dumb husband in the background. What had caused the dumbness, he could not possibly imagine, but no one stayed dumb for fun.

The affair was over, if it had even amounted to that. He was too old. Marianne had spoiled him and shielded him from the outside world, but at the same time deprived him of all defences. He wasn't up to coping with an unknown woman. He doubted he would even dare to be alone with her.

As always when he was out of sorts, he took refuge with Ellen. He had done that for as long as he could remember – with some interruptions. There had been long periods in his life when he did not need her. And even longer periods when she didn't have time for him. Marianne had never really understood how strong his ties to Ellen were. 'Bo and his aunt!' she would say, and shake her head. There was a little jealousy and with some justification. He had always been in love with Ellen, albeit in different ways and under different circumstances. Now he felt mostly affection and concern for her. He had realised that she would not be around for ever and that was a weight on his heart. He had already lost Marianne. In all probability, Ellen would be next. He wondered if he had embarked on his rash correspondence with Anna to protect himself against the impending void.

He has never said anything about her to Ellen, as she would not understand. She wasn't the kind of person who would have needed to resort to a Personal ad. Admirers had come in hordes and those who were still alive continued to come tottering round. '*Ach*, those old men!' she sometimes said, as though she were speaking about annoying flies.

He still thought briefly about telling her of his weakness

for her. He loved to hear her laugh. But he was not sure how she would react. She didn't listen now like she had before. She seemed to be withdrawing into her own world. She was still very clear-headed but to tell the truth, perhaps not as interested in things as she had previously been.

She had become so fragile, he wished that there was someone with whom he could share responsibility for her. Someone who could keep an eye on her and arrange for home care and transport and whatever. After all he was only a man and what could he do if one day he had to change her nappies? She often asserted that she was not incontinent, 'not in the least', and that in itself made him suspicious.

But there wasn't anyone else. She had never been married and never had children. Her freedom was too precious. She had been born free, virtually an orphan from the beginning, she claimed. That was obviously untrue. She had been motherless from birth, but never fatherless; even if the father had had little interest at the beginning in the new-born but had handed her over to her sisters' care. Three healthy young women should be able to take care of a baby without bothering him.

The eldest of the three sisters had become Bo's own mother almost a decade later. It had caused a scandal that slowly broke the Old Man. An unexplained scandal, which not even Ellen was able to get to the bottom of. But not before the old man had been buried, had Bo been acknowledged and brought home in measured triumph. Freedom after their father's oppression had made the sisters almost bold and there was a great deal of pent-up tenderness and love that could finally be unleashed. But freedom came too late. They were inhibited and insecure – the biological mother not least – and though they wanted nothing more than to give him a good home,

43

they did not quite know how to go about it. As an adult, he never doubted their good intentions.

He had almost no memory of his earliest days. Everything was just confusion. To begin with, he was not sure who his real mother was, although she had visited him in Älvsjö. But he could not see any difference between her and her sisters. All three were tall and thin with pale faces and small grey protruding eyes. They all spoke loudly and clearly. The old man had been not only bad-tempered but also hard of hearing. They handled the boy awkwardly with cold hands and were hurt when he withdrew from their unsure grasp.

It was Ellen of course who saved him from being choked by constant warnings, thick clothes and clumsy attentions. He could never understand how she could also be an aunt. She was just a schoolgirl. The others were hopelessly old. He and Ellen were children who belonged together, both orphans (even though he had a mother and she had a father) in a world of pale clumsy spinsters.

Without Ellen he would never have made the necessary adjustments. She was the most important person in his life. But she wasn't motherly in any way. She took him out with her as soon as he came home from school and encouraged in him all the despised Älvsjö bad habits. They swore in competition. It was she who taught him, not the other way round. Frozen and snivelling he hung around with her in Gärdet and on the streets, was looked at askance by her boyfriends, sometimes abandoned in some dreary backyard but always taken back into favour again. 'He's my little brother,' she said, apologising for him. 'I can't go out without him.'

Afterwards she brushed him down at the door so that snow and dirt flew about, and wiped his nose before she took him into the entrance-hall. They were almost always met with a scolding. Ellen, because she had missed lessons. Where had they been? What had they been up to? And how could Bo have got himself so horribly dirty? Other six-year-olds could go out and play without coming back looking like little pigs. Why did he always come home in such a state?

They were too old, his mother and his aunts, to take on a little child again, and a boy into the bargain. In spite of everything Ellen had been easier, even if the Old Man spoiled her more and more every year. Responsibility for a boy was too heavy for them. They were already fixed in their ways.

He didn't understand why he was thinking about all that just now. He seldom allowed his thoughts to wander back to those days. When Marianne plied him with questions, he always said that he had no memory of his childhood. But you can't have suppressed everything, she persisted. If you don't work on your memories you will never reconcile yourself with your childhood. That way you will never grow up, she declared. She so much wanted him to tell her everything.

But he just couldn't and that wounded her. He continued to keep his memories to himself, even at the risk that he would never grow up.

It must have been the unhappy correspondence with Anna and his concern about Ellen that had caused this tumult in his head. He had slept badly, troubled by wild dreams. Long dead people kept on appearing. But he couldn't perceive any clear significance in the dreams, not even the simplest message.

He never dreamed about Marianne whom he constantly missed, only about his dead mother and his dead aunts. There was no obvious explanation for it.

He unlocked the outer door of Ellen's apartment high up

on Styrmans Street and found to his relief that the security screen was open, so that he avoided having to tussle with two locks. The television was on, something American so far as he could tell from the sound. She was sleeping soundly in front of it in a comfortable armchair with her legs stretched out on the footrest and covered by a plaid blanket. Just her feet were sticking out clad in leather boots. The sight cut him to the quick. She had always been careful about what she put on her feet. High-heeled shoes, elegant indoor styles... and then suddenly sheepskin slippers in a concession to old-age's swollen blue toes. But in other ways she'd maintained her former elegance. A silk blouse, something shiny in the ears, her hair light and fluffy like a meringue, and the waft of expensive perfume surrounded the sleeping figure. Her head had sunk forward and her chin lay at an uncomfortable angle to her shoulders.

A wave of affection swept over him when he looked at her. She had become so small and defenceless, she who in spite of her unpredictability had once been his only security. He put off the television – she didn't notice anything. Her hearing-aid was lying on the table beside her. And also her glasses. She was now more or less deprived of two senses. He wondered if she remembered to take her medicines at the right times. Some jars and a half-empty water glass stood on a little tray. He didn't know of what use they were. She was reluctant to talk about her health, or rather her ill-health. He didn't even know whether there was actually anything wrong with her, or if it was just a matter of the machinery beginning to wear out.

The fact that she could no longer manage to keep things in order had been obvious for a long time. He reluctantly began to pick up after her. Newspapers had fallen on to the floor, there were books lying on the sofa and glasses containing a few murky dregs stood everywhere. She put them down wherever she happened to be standing and then forgot about them. She needed to have someone coming in every day, someone to look after her on a regular basis. He must sort out that problem for her. So far he had only arranged for the occasional person to come in, but he was always willing to act as her chauffeur and drive her on different errands. He waited outside the hairdresser, carried bags from System[14] and the covered market, fetched her from the gym and delivered her to various lunch appointments, Sometimes they went to the theatre together and occasionally to an exhibition. On Saturday evenings they had dinner together if she didn't have a more attractive invitation.

'You are very good to your old aunt,' she sometimes said and patted his arm. But the look she gave him had a sting in it. She had not become humble or grateful in her old age. She took all the help she was given as only her due. She had been spoiled all her life but very little protected.

He took the glasses out to the kitchen. There wasn't an inch of empty space to put them down. All the surfaces were occupied. Nothing had been put away. There was a musty smell and he opened the window before he began to put things in the already half-filled dishwasher. There were messy plates with the remains of a meal, knives and forks which she had just put down anywhere! He couldn't understand how someone so smart and well-groomed as Ellen was could live in such a disgusting mess.

But she had always been like that. He remembered her room when she was a girl; everything all over the place: film magazines under the bed in untidy heaps, lipstick and mascara stuck under a dictionary, clothes everywhere, clean and dirty mixed up together. The sisters didn't dare to say anything. She had a dreadful temper.

He heaved a sigh and opened the refrigerator. It was full to bursting. There was a sour smell of things going off on the shelves. He filled two carrier bags with packets bearing long-past sell-by dates, unidentifiable remains of different kinds of salad, every possible kind of dip, mouldy liver paste and mouldy cheeses. And finally soft furry carrots, a rotten cucumber and withered brown streaked lettuce. She must have lost her judgment to have thought she could eat all that on her own!

He became increasingly depressed as he stood in the messy kitchen, but he didn't give up. Marianne had made sure that he was able to carry out simple household tasks. For example, he knew that a floor had to be properly swept before one washed it. He gritted his teeth and made a start. Afterwards he saw with a certain satisfaction that the water under the lather was dark brown.

He didn't go into her bedroom. That would have overstepped the bounds. He had no desire to deal with her strewn around underclothes, blouses and stockings. Nor did he feel like cleaning the bathroom and toilet. It was too intimate. He didn't want to know more about her slovenliness than he already knew. During their long marriage, Marianne had impressed upon him that one should never leave a ring of dirt around the bath tub after having a bath. The same thing naturally applied to the hand basin. Ellen had lived untouched by such scruples. He sighed as he stood on the bathroom carpet

On the side of the hand basin there was a mug of scummy blue water. He looked into it apprehensively. Under the furry surface lurked the rubber crescent of a denture. 'Good God!' he thought in shock, 'Not that as well.' He had never known that her teeth were not her own. The discovery made him unspeakably sad. Slippers, hearing aids, glasses, false teeth, and disorder all around her. Everything suggested deterioration. How could he possibly put all this right.

Then Ellen suddenly woke up, caught sight of him and lit up. She looked more squirrel-like than ever. She had benefited from the rest.

'I'm glad you turned off the television. It was an awful film,' she said, a little thickly, while she fumbled with her hearing aid. Next it was the turn of the spectacles and then she suddenly realised that there was something missing.

She put her hand in front of her mouth and giggled, surprisingly undisturbed in spite of everything. It seemed that for her it was only a practical matter rather than something to be ashamed of. It surprised him, because she had always been careful about her appearance. But he quickly understood. She thought of him as her little brother, not as a grown man. It was he who had more difficulty in accepting the passage of time than she did. His Ellen should be for ever irresistible.

'I had such a crazy dream last night!' he said when she came back from the bathroom with rouge on her cheeks, colour on her lips and her teeth in place. 'I dreamed that it was my birthday and we had a children's party at home.'

She raised her eyebrows in surprise. They rarely spoke about his childhood. Neither of them had much inclination to revisit those memories. When they occasionally compared their recollections they never remembered the same things. It was hard to believe that they had grown up in the same family and apartment.

'Mama sat at the piano and played, Elsa clapped her hands and tried to get us to hold each other's hands and play ring games. The strange thing was that I was grown up but suffering in the same way as when I was little. But the guests were children and they sulked. I was ashamed for Mama, for Elsa and Hildur, but you didn't seem to be there.

'They were dreadful parties,' said Ellen with her malicious little smile. 'The girls had no idea how one should create a festive mood. They were doomed from the beginning. But you should have been at *my* children's parties. There was a fishing pond, a magician in a tall hat and ice-cream with green candy-floss… no expense spared. "What must be, must be". That was the Old Man's slogan. He was proud of me. The girls were so ugly, so dreadfully ugly.'

It amused him that she still called her three sisters 'girls'. It sounded so old-fashioned. She definitely didn't count herself as one of them. And no one else did either. There were the girls and Ellen. But he had had enough of memories and regretted that he had ever mentioned his dream. It was usually a mistake to bring up how things were. It left a feeling of emptiness, of never having really fitted in. Ellen wasn't particularly tactful either. It was far from the first time she had wounded him.

He felt relieved when a little later he was on the way to Fältöverst with a list in his hand. He had to go to the pharmacy and the book-shop, change the library book, and then on to ICA[15] for fruit, frozen food and something from the delicatessen counter.

It was still only one o'clock. He had plenty of time.

★

50

At ten minutes to three he was standing outside NK. He decided he wasn't going to make himself known to Anna, just scout around a bit and check her out, but to his shame he felt brighter than for a long time, almost adventurous. He stood up straight and breathed deeply.

NK was an excellent place for a rendezvous. The entrance hall was like a beehive with people swarming in and out. But even before he was in the atrium his childhood feelings of inadequacy returned. It was here that he'd been brought as a child by his mother and aunts. They liked to go and look around the big store. And they were critical. It was as if the Old Man's little metal badge with his account number on it gave them a self-confidence that others lacked. Only refined people had an account at NK. In his memory he saw himself dragging after his mother with her hand holding tightly on to his, while she chose what he should have. Then he had to try on the new clothes in front of a mirror with her standing in the background. He stood there looking pale and limp, almost exhausted, while she for once looked rosy in the cheeks and eagerly pointed at the seams which were puckered and the trouser legs that had to be taken up. The alteration seamstress crouched on the floor with a mouth full of pins and the black-clad sales assistant smiled at him haughtily. It was extremely embarrassing and he was ashamed of himself and his miserable expression but even more ashamed that he'd let down his mother, who had arranged it all. He just wanted to get out.

It suddenly struck him that it was absolute madness to have chosen NK as a meeting place. He had never been happy here. Mostly he'd trailed around half-dead from the heat and lack of oxygen, and having to seem grateful for garments which he had never asked for and hadn't chosen. And it hadn't got any better with the passage of time. The ventilation seemed to be as defective as ever. The only thing that could be said in defence of his suggestion was anonymity. One could easily disappear in the crowd. In the interests of safety he had left his pre-agreed Loden coat hanging at home and was wearing a rather sporty jacket and a tweed hat instead. In those clothes he hoped he would be safe from Anna's sharp eyes.

He would just check out the area, nothing more, and take the opportunity to buy some small things for the girls since he was already there. He strolled around the atrium and was continually pushed and shoved when he distractedly picked up some stockings from the heap – he seemed to have ended up in hosiery – very colourful in red and green. Perhaps there was something here suitable for Louise? As he passed through he looked up at the cafeteria and was almost alarmed. He hadn't remembered that it was so big and that the tables were so close to one another. How could he possibly find Anna in that crush? What surprised him most was that so many young, or perhaps fairly young women had the time and means to sit there in the middle of the day. There were fewer men, but not so few that he would be conspicuous if he found a vacant table. Which he obviously had no intention of doing.

On closer examination he saw that there were also lots of older women at the tables. Well-dressed and groomed, they'd decided to take a rest during their shopping trip. Large NK bags occupied free chairs and leaned against table legs. He didn't dare to look more closely at them for fear of staring right into the face of a white-haired woman in a beige poplin coat with her hair tied up in a knot. In his imagination she had grown into a huge enlargement of Tekedsgumman.[16] But why should she have kept to the agreement when he hadn't?

Which of those women of more mature years could be her? Which of them would – to the extent that she was guided by her intuition – get up from her chair and call out: 'Here I am, Bo!'

It was a frightening thought and he went quickly past the cafeteria. Nothing happened and no one tried to hail him. Relieved but feeling somewhat breathless, he couldn't help looking back. And there she sat! At the back against the wall and at a table for one. She had thick white hair, was wearing a dark blue jacket and a plaid skirt – a very elegant woman – and in spite of the distance it seemed as though she was following him with her eyes. But she didn't make the slightest attempt to make further contact. Perhaps she didn't notice him at all, perhaps it only seemed like that.

He fled up the escalator in a panic.

He was not ready to make himself known. Not yet at least.

Obviously he had imagined that she was looking at him. She was just sitting there and resting with her thoughts far away.

He took the escalator right up to the restaurant and then walked slowly down, floor by floor. Meanwhile he decided to give Anna one more chance. This time he planned to pitch camp so that he could take the enemy from behind, so to speak. He would see without being seen.

He still had vague plans to find some presents for his daughters, but he was not concentrating and wandered around the various departments, filled with distaste for so much conspicuous consumption. He also became depressed at seeing himself again and again in various mirrors. At first he didn't even recognise himself – the person seemed only vaguely familiar. But when he stared at that familiar forehead wrinkled with suspicion he saw that it was indeed him. He had just seen himself as he must be seen by others, and not in the usual position in front of the hall mirror with his head held high and a strained expression on his face.

He had always had a good colour and an elastic gait. At least he had often heard that said of him, even if it was a long time ago. So it was almost a shock to see a pale grey stooping old man walking past in the mirror, wearing his clothes. He didn't want to acknowledge that old man, and thought that the jacket aged him. It was Marianne who had chosen it. 'That's exactly what you need,' she had said. 'A light warm jacket of good quality and at a reasonable price.' He himself would have chosen a suede jacket, but she ruled that out. Now he was sure that it was that unusually warm jacket that made him look so hunched at the shoulders. The Loden coat would have been better. He would remember that next time he went on an adventure.

So he stood on the stairs above the cafeteria again and quickly looked over to see whether the lady in the blue jacket was still there. She wasn't. Disappointment warred with relief. She had been a stylish woman, but perhaps not his type. 'Good riddance!' he thought to himself. He often turned to English when he was upset. It had a calming effect and he had a store of favourite phrases from crime novels.

The tables were still full. There were more couples than before and also more older women. His glance fell on a woman alone who was reading, while absent-mindedly lifting up a coffee-cup. She was completely absorbed in her book. He liked what he saw. That soft profile – the tip of her nose was pleasantly rounded. Her light grey hair curved under at the neck in the way girls wore it when he was young. He thought it was called a page-boy cut. Ellen had worn her hair like that. Marianne as well. Both looked pretty with that style. She was wearing a grey dress, a little darker than her hair and in a soft material, and as far as he could see she had a fine body. Her shoulders and arms were thin, but her legs, which could only just be seen under the table had surprisingly strong calves. That would fit Anna's description, as she seemed to be always walking the dog. The woman made a thoroughly pleasant and cultured impression. She looked right in these surroundings which could be a problem. Anna had warned him that she was never 'correct', whatever she meant by that. He wanted it to be her anyway. The age was right and the book also gave him a hint. What could be more natural than that Anna should shelter behind a book while she waited for him?

Suddenly his heart started beating faster. Clearly he was more emotionally involved than he had thought. But it wasn't the usual fluttering of the heart that he was experiencing. It wasn't at all unpleasant, just a bit more noticeable. Suddenly he began to think about *Jan i Skrolycka*,[17] but he wasn't as deeply frozen as that. He had after all lived all his life among his nearest and dearest. Whatever it was, he would walk around a bit until he calmed down again.

She was still reading when he came back but then she lowered her book and looked at the entrance of the atrium as if she were waiting for someone. Then she lifted the book up again. She wasn't playing games, she seemed to be entirely unaware of him. He was almost ready to approach her. But he couldn't just go ahead. He had to be sure.

He walked around for a bit longer while he pondered on it. His heart rate had increased again. It couldn't be good for him, all that excitement. To divert his thoughts he went up to a cosmetics counter and bought an expensive jar of face cream. The package gave him an alibi. His heart calmed down.

When he went back she had gone. He couldn't understand how she could disappear so completely. Unless she had in fact seen him and taken the opportunity to slip away downstairs. In that case it was he who hadn't measured up. He had been discarded, cut up, flushed away and now he could go home.

He wandered gloomily out onto the street and then he saw her again. Now she had company – a young mother with a child's pram. They were obviously mother, daughter and grandchild. She looked happy and chatted eagerly with her daughter who looked very much like her. Although he was almost within touching distance of her, she didn't notice him.

Well at least he hadn't been rejected. He was filled with a certain confidence again and he looked at the time. A few minutes before half past three. A final attempt then, he thought, inwardly giving up the battle for lost already.

There was a quick turnover at the café tables. There weren't many who were still sitting there that he recognised from his previous visit and these he had already dismissed as impossible. But now he saw, with a sinking heart, a lone person placed strategically at a corner table. She had put a beige coat over the back of an empty chair near her. A green scarf lay on top of it and she had grey-streaked hair tied up on top of her head with a crinkly ribbon of the kind which made him think of a cancan girl's garter. His daughters used to put their hair up with such ribbons when they were teenagers. Blond wisps of hair always came loose and waved in the wind against their suntanned necks and cheeks. Their necks were so thin and their cheeks so downy! They were irresistible in summer, his daughters.

On an older woman that hairstyle looked careless and unbecoming, particularly if the neck beneath was thin and stringy. Otherwise there were no significant faults in her that he noticed. She looked the type to dig a garden plot, take the dog for a walk and frighten a man into silence. But she also looked so very sad.

Hardly a prize. He might be old and careworn himself but he wasn't that desperate. He still wanted the best or nothing at all.

He looked at her again and this time she became aware of it and met his glance with suspicion and dismissal in her eyes. He thought that she visibly recoiled though that was probably an exaggeration. He hadn't imagined that Anna would be like that! He turned down the stairs again, went up to the stocking counter and bought a pair of red and green striped tights and had them wrapped up. He had no idea which of the girls would want them, but his two packages would make him look like an ordinary father of a family thinking about Christmas.

At the exit he sneaked a last look at the cafeteria and felt certain that he was being watched. The person with the tied-up hair had been joined by a lady in a hat. He had glimpsed that hat a few times before moving between the cosmetics counter and the jewellery section. He had noticed it but dismissed it as being unthinkable for Anna. The hat's jaunty angle over the forehead in no way fitted with his impression of the woman who had written so many melancholy letters to him.

But now he was suddenly unsure. The lady in the hat had sat down on the empty chair next to the sad woman. Obviously it didn't mean that they were in collusion, although they could be. But they seemed to get on well together. He looked one last time at their table and unexpectedly met an amused look from under the hat. The distance involved was considerable and perhaps he had only imagined that it was amused. Whether he had or not, he felt thoroughly disturbed. He strode quickly to the exit with those eyes burning into his back. He felt that he had given himself away.

But a bit later he realised how naïve and absurd he was being. One doesn't meet the woman of one's dreams through an advertisement placed in the Personal column. He should have realised that from the beginning instead of allowing his expectations to get out of hand. The only things that had caused it were the loss of Marianne and his worries about Ellen. In recent months he had seen the onslaught of old age on her. It was like a dress rehearsal for the process that would soon affect him too. Nobody was safe. But it would also be some time before he became a grubby old man who shuffled around in slippers and didn't know whether it was day or night. Before the worst overcame him, he had hoped to meet a welcoming and attractive woman to share his company sometimes.

Lost to reality, he should have realised that his more pressing problem at the moment wasn't putting an end to his loneliness, but seeing to it that Ellen was properly looked after. He owed her that. The whole dragged out correspondence with Anna, culminating in his humiliating flight, was just a distraction, an excuse to avoid dealing with a serious problem.

But who would ever want to put their first love in an institution?

Håkan was sitting at the kitchen table with the newspaper in front of him. Advent candles shone in the window. Outside it was drizzling. The sky was hanging low over field and lake. There was a little white powder on the verges of the road but it was quickly being washed away by the rain. Fabian was sleeping on his back in his basket, with his front paws in the begging position and his little browny-pink stomach exposed.

'I'm going out now,' she said. 'Don't expect me back until supper time. I think I will try and find some Christmas presents while I am in town.'

He didn't answer or even look up from his newspaper but when she was backing the car out of the garage he looked at her through the window. Sometimes he just listened to the sound of the engine. He heard if something was wrong with it so much more easily than she did. She waved but he didn't acknowledge it and she hadn't expected that he would. By saying nothing he let her know that he thought her journey completely unnecessary. The publishers could easily have sent the book by post like they usually did. As always she was in his bad books when she went out into the world. Just by looking at her without changing his expression he could give her a bad conscience. Without having any idea of her real plans he'd succeeded in making this journey feel shameful and illicit.

In the car she felt free, although no longer as free as she once did. Then it was as if she forgot that she had to go home again. Now she regarded herself as a privileged prisoner out on licence. But the prison was also her home. She didn't want to live anywhere else; nowhere else would suit her better.

One of the most enjoyable aspects of the car was the radio. She could sit there and change programmes when she wished without disturbing anybody. Håkan was sensitive to noise. It was no wonder the children had been in a hurry to leave home.

She emptied her head of thoughts and listened to P1[18] while she drove along the old winding roads towards the E18. There wasn't much traffic on the road and the miles ticked by. The drizzle unexpectedly changed to a mixture of sleet and big wet snowflakes, and then just as abruptly stopped. After Bålsta the traffic became heavier. The journey took on another rhythm but now she had hymns to buoy her up. It felt as though there was a host of guardian angels sitting in the back seat. In addition she had had her licence for over fifty years and thought she had a certain flair for driving.

'Do you still drive into the centre?' asked elderly country folk incredulously. Advanced driving is automatically called into question when a woman reaches seventy or more. But men were obviously different. She had never heard anyone query Håkan's continuing to drive into Stockholm. His mental state had often been discussed among the neighbours, never his ability to drive.

She was aware that she was beginning to be a bit stubborn about this determination to drive for as long as she still had her wits. But the question was, would she know when it was time to stop? Or would she go on unaware until something dangerous happened.

In the centre she missed a slip road and was obliged to go round and round for quite a while before she found her way and could park in the visitors' bay at the back of the publishing house. When she was in the lift she suddenly became nervous and pinched her cheeks to give herself some colour and look healthy. The light fell mercilessly on her lines and wrinkles. She looked barely capable of work.

But when a little later she came down again she felt almost ridiculously elated. No one seemed to have considered her feeble. She looked forward to carrying on doing a good job quickly and reliably. She hadn't been put on the shelf as she had feared in recent weeks. And the new novel which she would be working on wasn't too long or too dense. She put it lovingly on the back seat and took out a large plastic bag.

The happiness stayed with her while she walked down Drottning Street. The crowds and the signs of Christmas were a stimulating contrast to her silent everyday life on the narrow forest paths with her husband and dog. She felt like indulging in a lot of treats. It would soon be Christmas and she would buy something amusing and unexpected for Simon and Emma, even though she remembered the overfilled toy-cupboard in their room. But at the entrance to Stor & Liten[19] she had already changed her mind. It was so overwhelmingly commercialised that she didn't want anything to do with it.

Something for Håkan then to silence her conscience, which since the first letter to Bo had had been pricking her uncomfortably? A dressing-gown? His old one had some curious bald patches but she had never heard him express any desire for a new one, not even during the time when he was still speaking. A nice sweater would be safer.

But actually she wanted to get something for herself. It

was a long time since she had gone window-shopping and now she really wanted to buy something special. Particularly now that she was going to NK – and she definitely was – and had plenty of time.

She sat down in the powder room, right at the top next to Bobergs restaurant, put down her bag and took stock of her hat. She had been given it by Malin, who sometimes went shopping in a hurry and then passed the results over to her mother. But Anna was not really a hat person and had never worn it. Now she finally had a use for it and she put it on and looked critically at herself in the mirror. It was an expensive but pretty hat. It gave her a slightly adventurous look but also a certain elegance. She scarcely recognised herself and twisted and turned her head quizzically in front of the mirror. It required self-confidence to carry it off. She barely managed it because it was the kind of hat which would eventually end up in the dressing-up cupboard. It was ideal if you didn't want to be recognised. She couldn't imagine that Bo would make any connection between his country penfriend and something so showy. It wasn't her usual style, which must somehow have appeared between the lines she wrote.

In that hat she could stride confidently into the crowd in NK among the other women without fear of being detected. She didn't want to go home without knowing what he looked like, her old archivist. Then they would see what happened next. Or rather *if* anything more were to happen.

Half an hour later when she went down the steps towards the gallery café her coat was open. Underneath glowed a new red jumper with a polo-neck. She hadn't been able to resist it and didn't remember when she had last felt so pleased with something she had bought. It looked pretty against her grey overcoat. She sneaked a look in each mirror she passed and every time was surprised anew. Life had come into her face. Her cheeks looked softer than usual in the shadow of the hat brim and her long thin mouth looked a little playful.

'Silly old thing,' she chided herself. But she was actually quite pleased. Not every woman her age went around in disguise looking for an unknown man on a weekday in NK.

She had a large NK carrier bag in her hand containing some small things she'd picked up as she went along. Socks with comic patterns on them for Simon and Emma, practical and astonishingly expensive woollen socks for Håkan – there hadn't been a suitable sweater this time. And obviously the blouse and cardigan which she bought for herself. All these things filled out the bag so that, against her better judgment, she felt as though she had a right to be there among the well-dressed NK big spenders. She entered into the role so easily that she stood for a long time in front of a display of earrings as if she were really thinking of buying something.

Bo would hardly be looking for her among the jewellery and cosmetics. She can't have shown any tendency to vanity in her letters. He would obviously be waiting for her to sit down in the cafeteria, straight up and down in a beige poplin coat, just waiting to be seen.

But she didn't do that. Secure under her hat, she went round the usual departments and felt, in her red jumper, a part of the Christmas display while she let her eyes wander over the people coming the other way. She was sure of one thing. He was not sitting alone and waiting at a table in the cafeteria. But she hadn't expected that he would leave himself so exposed. He wasn't that desperate to meet her. Exactly as she meant to, he would leave himself a line of retreat.

But he must be somewhere… Most of the men in here seemed to have female company and they looked generally more tired and worn out than the few who were walking around on their own. Anna was surprised. So many bald heads, so many furrowed brows and so many well-cut coats. She couldn't remember when Håkan had last had an overcoat. He didn't go to the theatre or to funerals.

She looked again but couldn't see anyone who fitted the picture she had of her penfriend. She had imagined that she would instinctively recognise him but there were no vibrations in the air suggesting that he was in the vicinity. That surprised her. It was now eighteen minutes past three. She had been sure that he would arrive in good time.

Then her heart gave a jump. A grey-haired gentleman was standing on the stairs and earnestly scanning the throng. He was tall and upright. One couldn't avoid seeing him. She stood and watched. Then his eyes lit up and he raised his hand. For one astonishing moment she really believed that it was *him* and that he immediately thought that it was *her*, but then she realised that his greeting was intended for a woman right behind her. The breath went out of Anna in a rush. You can't always assume you will win the first prize and what would she have done with a man who seemed so at home in another world, in another class, among those beautiful, if also aged, people.

Still, the woman whose cheek he had just very lightly kissed, looked fairly ordinary; certainly well-dressed and well-shod but nothing special. Probably living in a country manor with the breeding of hunting dogs as a hobby and a pug-dog for company. Perhaps horses in the stable.

Time passed. There were no longer any gentlemen of the

right age sitting alone in the cafeteria. It was obvious that he was as frightened of showing himself as she was. But she was beginning to wonder about a man in a beige jacket and a brown herringbone tweed hat. He seemed suspiciously interested in the cafeteria and at the same time keen not to be seen from it. He looked around as though on the point of launching an ambush, but now and then he walked around only to quickly go back again. He hadn't noticed her. His glance had just passed her by.

She studied him carefully. He was only a little taller than her but then she was tall, and he was a bit round-shouldered. There was something slightly withdrawn about him as though he hadn't been mixing with other people for some time. He wasn't wearing a Loden coat or a cap but why should he keep to the agreement when she hadn't? He had a good colour in his face but she found in difficult to imagine him gliding over black ice. Possibly he had lied a little about his cross-country skiing to make himself interesting; perhaps he did kick-sledding instead. It was safer but not something one bragged about. She could very well imagine him kicking comfortably over the ice with his lunch bag on the seat.

He was clearly interested in a lady in the restaurant. The light was falling softly on her shining grey pageboy haircut. She looked pleasant and was wearing a nice outfit. The book in her hand reinforced the impression of an educated lady. Anna was satisfied that he had chosen that person, although neither the clothes nor the haircut accorded with her own hints about her appearance. That showed that he had some aspirations, that he expected something beyond an ordinary septuagenarian.

It was strange that the person in question did not realise that she was being watched. It was obviously a very good book. But he in turn did not realise that Anna was watching him. And now she could see that his features were stronger than she had at first thought. There was nothing feminine about him. Perhaps she had been expecting something of that kind, because he had talked about his many aunts and showed such affection for the very elderly Ellen. Ridiculous how much one can embroider the few facts one has. She wondered what picture he in turn had built up of her. Suddenly she wasn't at all sure that it was Bo and felt rather silly. She went round the jewellery section again and when she came back he had disappeared. The lady with the book was paying in the café. Then she hurried down to meet a young mother in the atrium, smiling as she bent over the pram and kissing her daughter on the cheek. It was clear that it was her daughter. There was an invisible aura of warmth surrounding them. Anna felt a stab of pain in her heart. Malin never came to meet her with babies in a pram.

Then nothing more happened. He had given up and gone away. Their gazes had never met. She herself had suddenly lost heart. There was no longer anything to induce her to reveal herself. And in any event, she no longer needed him now that she had a couple of months of secure work in front of her. But that happiness had also petered out. She had waited too long and worked up an expectation of not getting anything new. She even regretted buying the red jumper. What would she do with it? No one would see it and it had been ridiculously expensive.

It was already dark outside. The journey back would be traffic jams all the way to Bålsta and then mile after mile of dark country roads. She didn't like driving in the dark. She was blinded by the oncoming traffic and felt insecure. She suddenly felt so tired that she went into the cafeteria and sat down at the nearest and best free place. She ordered a cup of black coffee and then looked around. The woman on the other side of the table had been sitting there for a while, and the amusing thing was that she could easily have passed for Anna's description of herself, with her little straggly bun in a scrunchy and her beige coat. A Swedish old lady in all her modesty – insignificant and boring. She looked unmarried. Perhaps she was a retired librarian, a bit anxious and withdrawn. Bo had only given her a fleeting glance as far as Anna could see. Perhaps it was a little wrong of her and perhaps she just needed to hear a pleasantry but Anna smiled at her across the table and said something about the crowds and Christmas shopping.

She received a surprisingly friendly smile in return and the woman leaned forwards confidingly across the table.

'I like sitting here and looking at the people,' she said. 'They are such an elegant crowd and I never tire of wondering about their backgrounds, what kind of work they do and how they live.'

'I know,' said Anna who had just been indulging in such speculation, 'I'm the same.'

'I am puzzled by that man there by the hosiery counter. Don't look now… I think he feels that he is being watched. He looks respectable and presentable enough. There is definitely nothing unpleasant about him, but yet he must be on some shady expedition because he seems so nervous. He has been hovering about for quite a while now.'

Even before Anna got to see him, she knew it was her old Bo who was making himself conspicuous. He looked abandoned, almost touching.

'He is definitely not dangerous,' she said and couldn't

help smiling. She felt secure, almost invisible, now that she had company. This conversation was certainly absurd but not entirely inaccurate.

Then Bo lifted his head and seemed to be looking straight at her. It felt as if he were looking her in the eye. The distance was considerable but she sure she wasn't mistaken. Then he hurried over to the exit. His back was straight and he walked stiffly as if he were expecting a poisoned arrow to land between his shoulder-blades. He was clearly deeply offended.

But he could not possibly have heard a single word of the conversation! It must have been simply her expression or perhaps her companion's undisguised interest that drove him to take flight.

'I wonder what came over him? He was in a real hurry.'

Anna didn't answer, but just shook her head dismissively. Then she slowly took off her hat and fluffed up her hair with her fingers. She didn't need the hat any more. Whether it had done her a favour or not was difficult to say.

That wasn't something Bo wanted to do again. He didn't even want to think about it. In his anxiety he was angry with Ellen for the mess she had made even though he realised that it wasn't her fault. But it was just like her to leave the work to others. He thought she even smiled maliciously with one corner of her mouth while she was being carried down to the ambulance, although it was probably just because her face was lop-sided. But he couldn't be sure. There was a fundamental heartlessness in her character to which he had never reconciled himself.

Be that as it may, it was he who now had to clean, scrub, dry and rinse off – over and over again. What he couldn't understand was the quantity of blood. How could there have been so much of it? How could she have hurt herself so badly just struggling to get up! The telephone, which had been pulled down onto the floor, was as bloodied as the receiver which lay out of her reach. She had knocked over a couple of chairs and pulled the quilt and sheets off the bed and everything was covered in blood and soiled. One would have thought there had been a murder in the apartment, not that an old lady had fallen down and couldn't get up again. She looked dreadful as she lay there, his elegant haughty Ellen. She should have been spared that humiliation.

Obviously he should have gone round to her immediately when he started being worried that something was wrong, after the telephone had given the engaged signal for the whole evening. But the strong probability had been that she had not put the receiver back properly. That sometimes happened and then he went round and put it back on. But he couldn't sleep, troubled as he was and very upset by having been a figure of fun at NK. After the telephone had given the engaged signal four times he gave up, quickly washed, shaved and dressed and drove the car through the empty streets into town.

Ellen was lying on the floor by the bed, thoroughly frozen and almost unconscious. So small and thin, so desolate with her cold blue legs drawn up to her chest. And yet that pitiful little body in her rucked-up nightdress was so heavy that he couldn't manage to get her back onto the bed. All he could do was to lay the eiderdown over her and push a cushion under her head. Her white hair was stiff with dried blood but he couldn't see any wound.

Fortunately the ambulance came quickly and the two young paramedics took care of the stinking elderly lady as though it was the most natural thing in the world. He was seriously impressed by their professionalism.

'Now we are taking you to the hospital,' said one of them and gently stroked her cheek. 'Don't be afraid. Everything will be all right.'

And Ellen, who hadn't moved a muscle when he had tried to speak to her, responded to the touch with a little flutter of her eyelids and a twitch of the corner of her mouth. Bo was hurt. This was a new failure. All the concern and affection which he had shown did not give her a fraction of the reassurance the professional friendliness gave. She already looked less dead when they carried her out.

The ambulance had more than an hour's advantage on Bo when he got into the car to drive to the hospital in Danderyd. In the worst-case scenario she was still lying covered in blood in a corridor and in the best she had been showered clean and was lying in a freshly made bed with the standard issue yellow blanket over her. He didn't know what was wrong with her other than that it seemed life-threatening — was it a heart attack, a cerebral haemorrhage? Perhaps she needed an operation?

But when he finally found the right ward he discovered that she was waiting to be examined and didn't appear to be in immediate danger. He didn't feel particularly welcome. The night shift was just leaving and no one had time for him. He didn't persist in trying to see her but was in fact relieved to escape.

He drove home in the dark morning and was surprised at how heavy the traffic had suddenly become. It was several years since he had been out at this time on a winter morning. As a pensioner, one lives alongside but separate from real life until one is suddenly shaken out of one's comfortable existence.

While he drank his morning coffee in big greedy gulps his emotions suddenly caught up with him. He felt a heavy weight pressing down on him. How could he deal with all this? He was so afraid of anything to do with illness and hospitals. Marianne's death had increased that fear.

She'd seen that and teased him a bit about it. Above all, she'd made sure that he was not tormented unnecessarily and the girls really played their part. But now, afterwards, he felt sure that they had made him more helpless than he need have been even if it had been done out of loving consideration.

Louise was naturally without a job at that time and moved home to be near at hand. Ulrika and Karin took turns in relieving her. Up to the last week he only saw Marianne when she had been showered and made neat and tidy and was sitting by the window in her favourite chair with the telephone within reach. She stubbornly refused to let him help her to the toilet and got there on her own wobbly legs so long as they held her up.

And he was grateful to avoid washing and drying her. He couldn't bear to see her poor bony body. But the girls could. He could hear them laughing together in the bathroom. He couldn't understand the merriment.

They relieved him of all the heavy work. He wasn't to worry, he was told. Sometimes he felt that he didn't really belong there. But it was very important that he should listen to her plans for the future – his future, not hers. There was so much that had to be sorted out. Large, small and everything in-between — the sale of the house, which saucepans he should keep and which Louise should have. Marianne was very insistent that everything should be distributed fairly. How many forks against a small ring set with a sapphire?

She also planned her own death in some detail. She knew exactly what course things would take, what pain relief was available and what the alternatives were. She had also decided to die at home among her loved ones but with the support of all the professional help she could get. She wanted things to be calm and dignified. Music to listen to, flowers to rest her eyes on and the nearness of him and the daughters. And that's how it was. Afterwards everyone agreed that it couldn't have been done better.

Nonetheless he remembered the last days as being run like

an army camp. Louise, Karin and Ulrika were on their feet all the time, deathly tired but remarkably controlled and kindly towards the wide-eyed brood who continually stood at the slightly open door to Marianne's room. 'Is Grandma still alive, can we come in? We will be very quiet.'

In the kitchen there were small tempting dishes, which Marianne couldn't even look at. He had the impression that they were eating and drinking almost without interruption in those days, while the exhausted youngsters waited for their mothers. They did lessons at the dining-room table and played cards on the floor. Sometimes someone sat very gravely on his knee for a while. From time to time the sons-in-law turned up, both badly affected and dressed to face death. At best they took the children with them and disappeared.

Naturally he had moved out of the bedroom so that Marianne should have peace around her. His bed was still there but it seemed to be always occupied by one of the daughters or the grandchildren who fell asleep while on a visit. Every now and then it was used as a place to put down newspapers and books, which she would never manage to read and the large number of letters which she read with pleasure. She wanted him to read them as well. But he couldn't do it. They were too heart-rending. But Marianne kept her sharp sense of humour till the last and would giggle over some particularly flowery wording. She excused herself by saying said that it wasn't every day she found out how she was viewed by her friends.

Afterwards he allowed Ulrika to put her mother's bed in the small guest room. She was pleased. No one needed to know that Mama had lain dying in it, she said. All he could say in response was that Ulrika was just like her mother.

No, he couldn't trouble the girls with his worries about

Ellen. They had played their part and shouldn't be obliged to repeat it. He would have to manage by himself. Ellen was old. It was obvious that she would die. Perhaps that would be the best thing for her. She would avoid being a 'care package' with a withered face and an open mouth. And he would escape the huge responsibility and bad conscience of not visiting a 'care package' who no longer recognised him.

Then he realised that he was already using the past tense when he thought about her although it was the living Ellen who mattered now. He must ring the hospital and find out where they had put her and when he could speak to the doctors. And then he must make sure with his own eyes that she was being well looked after. He thought that it was all so difficult that it was almost impossible to deal with.

Marianne would have managed it quietly and efficiently. She was particularly good with doctors. Suddenly he fervently wished that she was still with him and could help him through all the difficulties which lay ahead. Above all he wished that she were still lying beside him in bed at night. Many times he regretted that he had given Ulrika her bed. He would have liked to have kept it for company.

Anna stood at the window with the watering-can in her hand and watched the car disappear around the corner by the oak-tree hill. Twice a year Håkan was summoned to a consultation with his doctor. While she gave the tired hibiscus a drop of water she wondered what the consultation was about. How much was Håkan revealing? Did he talk about the big problems or did he not let on about them – because he didn't want to, didn't have the strength or just couldn't. Did his doctor even know that this patient wasn't speaking to his wife and barely to anyone else? It was a long time since she had hoped that a visit to the doctor would lead to an improvement in him. In that way she had as little faith as Håkan in doctors and their ability to cure anything. Drugs which appeared to be very effective when she looked them up in FASS[20] rarely had a healing effect on him, but unfortunately did produce most of the negative side effects. They simply didn't do what they were supposed to do. The joy of living isn't something that one can recapture with medicine. As the years went by she had accepted that some depressions couldn't be affected by so-called happy pills. But Håkan was nevertheless responding in some ways to the treatment. He functioned like a completely normal person. He was very well-read, knowledgeable about politics and community affairs and very vigorous for his age. He liked walking in the woods and fields. In short, he functioned. He was neither confused nor lacking in judgment, though perhaps a bit absent-minded about things that didn't interest him. But he was fundamentally sharp and would certainly pass any cognitive tests with flying colours. The only things lacking in him were stamina and will. It was reasonable to assume that he would live for a long time. There was nothing that would wear him out except his inner world, which was closed to her.

Anna often wondered how great a part she herself had played in the big silence that enclosed him and knew that she was to some extent to blame. But it was all so complicated that she did not succeed in coming to any conclusion. A long time ago she had hardened her heart and washed her hands of the problem. Forty-five years of marriage had left some affection on her part plus a strong feeling of responsibility for him; on his side there was significant dependence. She was like a mother to an insecure five-year-old. She had to be within reach for him to be calm. She wasn't needed to act as company.

But she didn't want to be a mother to a seventy-four-year-old man. She couldn't feel like a mother to him. Her heart was like a hard nut. Its life's juices had dried up. She couldn't remember when she had last wept and there was scarcely a drop of humour left in her. In some ways she was as dull as him, although she didn't want to see it. She wondered if it had been noticeable in her letters and that was why Bo had run away and not been heard from since.

She was dried up – shrivelled and dried up and with a bitter taste.

But she was still useful as a translator and that skill hadn't deteriorated with age. When she worked, she felt fully alive.

It was a dark day but she liked the December darkness. She liked seeing the Advent candles in the farmhouse windows. They would shine at the edges of the woods and fields and she would shine back with candles set in the windows of both the kitchen and the living room. From her desk in her study she had a view over the oak-tree hill. She could see the headlights coming over the brow of the hill immediately before a car turned down it. They lived at the end of the road and she was not expecting any visitors. The postwoman had come and gone. Anna had at least four hours of welcome solitude in front of her. The telephone might ring. But Bo never rang her, even if he knew her number. He would not dare to disturb the married peace.

It was really dreadfully sad.

She sat down at her word processor and went over her work of the day before. She read and thought, made changes, thought and then changed things back. It was a kind of warming up to get herself going. The brain is slow to get moving like the cold motor of an old car which doesn't start when the key is turned in the ignition. It stayed fixed on problems though and often woke her in the middle of the night with a perfectly formed sentence which she was usually too tired to write down and then had forgotten in the morning. Or if she remembered it, was rarely perfect in the clear light of day.

Suddenly the telephone rang and her first thought was that something had happened to Håkan. She had been expecting it for years and it was a mystery that it had taken as long as it had, though his doctor hadn't expressed any such views on the matter. The roads were anyway full of alcoholics and drug users, speed merchants and those bent on suicide, other motorists who were senile or demented and above all ordinary drivers with no skill. In comparison to all of those Håkan appeared almost exemplary. And most of them got home for dinner every day without a dent in the car — which was itself almost a miracle.

Obviously the call was from the police or a hospital. But it was only Gertrud ringing and that meant a long call even if one didn't have time. Gertrud had a sixth sense and she could immediately tell from Anna's voice whether she was alone or not. They had been classmates for the whole of their school time and carried on being friends afterwards – except for a period when they were at high school when it was Gertrud and Håkan who were together. But he was replaced by a medical student.

Now Bengt had been dead for a couple of years but Håkan was still alive. Gertrud found it difficult to accept the unfairness.

Anna knew how conflicted she was in her affections when it came to Håkan. She envied Anna for still having him – even as he was now. Gertrud still had a soft spot for him in spite of everything, convinced that she'd been his great love. From time to time she made it clear to Anna that if only she – Gertrud – had remained with him, things would never have gone as badly awry with him as they had. And that his wife was perhaps not entirely free of blame.

Anna took from that as much as she wanted to.

But she knew that Gertrud missed her Bengt and found the loneliness difficult to bear. It was for this reason she rang so often. And now she had something to report. She had come straight from Danderyd Hospital where she had been visiting a cousin. Her marriage to Bengt, who in due course became a professor, had given her some specialist knowledge. She was inclined to consider herself the next best thing to a doctor and it was true that she had a certain intuition. She could immediately tell whether the prognosis was good or bad when she sat beside a sickbed.

Anne's view was that she sat beside sickbeds rather too often. Visiting the sick had become a kind of therapy for her loneliness. Gertrud scuttled from cancer to heart attack and spoke almost like a real doctor; in between visiting the sick, she listened patiently to all her old friends who had worries. And there were more and more of them. There was nothing strange about that. Life hadn't been particularly easy even when they were young. Now it had become worse and worse. Aching backs, rising rents, diabetes, shrinking widow's pensions, heart disease and varicose veins, green and grey cataracts — there was no end to the misery.

'So there I was, sitting by Anita,' said Gertrud. 'She is still paralysed and has difficulty communicating, but her eyes are speaking as Runeberg[21] would have said. It was heart-breaking. I sat there holding her hand when suddenly the curtain between the beds was drawn aside. And can you believe it – there was Ellen Rydeman in the other bed! White as chalk and with her sharp nose pointing straight into the air, but still with a certain radiance, if I can put it like that in such circumstances. Diaper and drip, as you can well imagine.'

Anna couldn't imagine it but no doubt in time she would experience those indignities for herself. The name didn't mean a thing to her.

'Ellen Rydeman,' repeated Gertrude with irritation. 'But you must remember her! Don't you remember how much we admired her, as young girls used to in the old days – passionately but from a distance.'

In contrast to Gertrud who had a phenomenal memory for people, Anna had difficulty with both names and faces – but something stirred in the dark depths of her memory.

'Ellen Rydeman? Don't you mean old Bojan?[22] Bojan, whom we treated so badly, until she cried and wrung her hands and threatened to fetch the principal.'

Anna could suddenly picture Ingeborg Rydeman clearly in front of her, at her raised desk with bible, psalter and prayer book. Tall and angular with her mild horse-like face, centre-parted and often unwashed hair hanging down her back in a long knot, pale and slightly protruding eyes, and non-existent discipline. And with that came a renewed twinge of bad conscience for all their giggling, whispering and general disobedience to her.

'No, not Bojan,' said Gertrud. 'Ellen, her younger sister. You must remember. The one that looked like a rose, with brown eyes and fair hair. We couldn't understand how they could be sisters. I worshipped her. And I could keep watch on her because we lived in Artilleri Street then, opposite the Rydemans. It was strange – just spinsters and Ellen. And then suddenly a little boy appeared, about the same age as me. That was before I began school; before you and I became best friends. There was something strange about a child suddenly appearing fully formed among them. There was gossip but I didn't really understand why, although I eavesdropped as much as I could.

'I don't remember anything about that,' said Anna. 'The only thing I do remember is that we were nasty to Bojan.'

'I don't remember that,' said Gertrud calmly. 'It was Ellen who fascinated me. I never played with the boy and when we moved to Grev Street I lost contact with them. But I carried on keeping a look out for Ellen and I was happy if I saw her in the schoolyard.'

'But we were cruel to Bojan,' repeated Anna. 'We almost plagued the life out of her, I think. Mostly out of pure stupidity, but still …'

'Rubbish. She was just impossible. Couldn't keep order.'

Gertrud said all that without batting an eyelid even though she was what Anna meant by a 'good person' – in spite of some peculiarities – with an infinite capacity for both listening and consoling.

'It was strange to see Ellen there in the bed. Old and frail. I even felt a little tearful because she had been such a captivating woman in her time, always surrounded by men. She never married or had children but kept a very expensive antiquarian shop in Sibylle Street. Bengt and I sometimes went to look at it, and occasionally bought something. It was something of a 'celebrity spot' at that time, although that expression wasn't used then. And she treated me like a valued customer although she didn't say so. By the way, do you remember what the boy was called? I don't.'

But Anna didn't think she had ever known it. She had never adored Ellen, just tormented poor Bojan, and she remembered that she had been the ringleader. That recollection upset her a lot and she quickly ended the conversation.

But later that evening Gertrude rang again.

'Bo!' she shouted in triumph. 'His name was Bo – Bo, not Bosse. Now I can sleep peacefully and hope you can do the same.'

But Anna couldn't sleep. There was something disturbing her. It had to do with Bojan and it wasn't just her own troubled conscience.

★

Over the next few days new reports on Ellen Rydeman streamed in. Gertrud watched her from the visitor's chair beside her cousin Anita as soon as there was the slightest gap in the curtain between the hospital beds. Ellen seemed to be on the way to recovery and even now in her feeble old age she received a lot of visits from male friends. From time to time Gertrud took an extra turn past Ellen's bed to get a closer look at them. Some had beards, one was clean-shaven, but they all brought boxes of chocolates and fruit. It was the clean-shaven one that Gertrud was most interested in. She thought this could be the boy, Bo, but because it was more than sixty years since she had last seen him it was difficult to be sure. The intimate and teasing tone between him and Ellen suggested they were related, but he obviously felt ill at ease in the hospital environment and literally turned pale at the sight of Ellen's varicose veins when a careless nurse forgot to close the curtain.

Gertrud was almost fixated on finding out about Ellen and her visitor. She excused herself by seeing it as a kind of compulsion. She had always been something of a 'Who's Who?' expert and memorised both people and names. But it had become much worse than that. Sometimes she wondered if it was actually normal to begin the day at six o'clock in the morning by looking at the death announcements in the social pages of *Svenska*.

Anna shrugged her shoulders. With the passing of the years it became more difficult to know what was normal and what wasn't. Everyone developed their own particular ways and rarely for the better.

Some days later Cousin Anita died from a new cerebral

haemorrhage. Gertrud was sad but not devastated. What kind of a life would Anita have had if she had survived? A blessing in disguise was that on her last visit Gertrud had been able to clarify that the clean-shaven visitor beside the next-door bed was who she thought he was. Ellen had dictated a full power of attorney for her nephew Bo Rydeman. Behind the curtain Gertrud had been all ears.

It was not a surprise to Anna, just confirmed her suspicions. She had already looked in the Stockholm directory and there was his name, address and telephone number. He lived in Hässelby a place washed by the waters of Lake Mälaren. But the knowledge that she had tormented his awful mother in almost all the religion lessons for two years was lying like a weight on her. And there was also the miserable conclusion to their planned meeting at NK.

'I wish that we hadn't been so cruel to Bojan,' she said once more.

'Don't keep going on about that. It happened a long time ago.'

Gertrud didn't seem to have the same recollections of Bojan as Anna had. In Anna's memory she was permanently standing on the podium in tears in front of the first row of pupils where Anna and Gertrud were sitting next to one another. She was so thin that her breastbone could be seen through her tight blouse; she didn't have breasts. What the girls found irresistibly funny was that the row of buttons on her blouse trembled when she breathed deeply. Then their hysterical giggling began and couldn't be stopped even though they bit their knuckles and bent double over the bench.

'We weren't any worse than the others,' Gertrud calmly pointed out. Her conscience was fairly clear.

But she hadn't exchanged letters with Bojan's son over the autumn months. And she would never get to know that Anna had done so. Her deep embarrassment and loneliness would be kept to herself.

But there was one question which she couldn't leave unasked.

'So what did Bo look like?'

'Very nice. There was nothing really wrong with him. And he didn't look in the least like the frightful spinsters. Nor like Ellen either come to that. Perhaps he was adopted after all.'

Anna was pleased with that answer. It confirmed her own impression of him. She had wondered for a while whether someone who had Bojan's blood in his veins would be worth knowing, particularly if he also looked like her. Now at least she knew that an objective viewer thought that he looked nice.

As the days went by, she thought about him more and more often. She didn't actually understand why. Nothing had happened to change things between them. But to her surprise she was beginning to use him as a conversation partner. She spoke to him a lot, without of course expecting a reply. Then she spoke for him. And she took trouble over what she said. She really wanted to entertain him at the same time as making a proper connection between them.

She found her new habit strange and slightly embarrassing but at the same time she derived unexpected pleasure from it. For the first time for many years there was someone who listened to what she said. Then she suddenly realised that the letter writing had become such a habit for her that she was suffering from withdrawal symptoms.

And so just before Christmas she sat down again at her writing desk.

Dear Bo,

Quite by chance I heard that your aunt Ellen is in Danderyd hospital. I am happy for your sake that she is getting better and hope that it won't be long before you will be having 'lunch with Ellen' again.

Our meeting at NK didn't stand a chance. We were both too cowardly and daren't even dress as we had promised. Instead we were sneaking around like children and spying on each other. That was really unworthy of two respectable old people. I think I guessed who you were – in a beige jacket and tweed hat? I hid myself under a hat with a brim – someone who always goes around bare-headed! Does that tell you something?

I wish you a Happy Christmas (although this letter won't reach you in time) and a Happy New Year.

She wrote her full name, Anna Ljung, at the bottom of the letter. On the reverse side she stuck a label with her address and telephone number. Then she placed the letter in an envelope and put stamps on it, looked thoughtfully at it and then pressed a plump little Father Christmas sticker to the opposite corner. She took Fabian with her and went out to put the letter in the post-box by the bus stop.

The anonymous times were over.

And she already regretted that before the letter hit the bottom of the post-box.

Dear Anna,

Thank you for the Christmas letter. When I recognised the type-
script it had the same effect on me as Christopher Robin's red
braces on Piglet. I was elated. I'd thought that we would never
hear from each other again and that it was too late for me to
have a new adventure even on a modest scale.

Obviously I am somewhat bewildered. Could your 'chance'
discovery of Ellen's condition be something to do with a stylish
lady with sharp eyes who often visited Ellen's room-mate at
Danderyd? She demonstrated an almost undisguised curiosity
about what was happening on our side of the curtain though she
was very obliging and polite to Ellen. She looked at me as well
every time she passed us – which happened a lot because her
own patient had the bed near the window and she had to go
past the foot of Ellen's bed to reach it. She had a lot of errands to
run! I couldn't understand why she was interested in us. Perhaps
she had known Ellen in former days. In her time my aunt was well
known, while I have always passed through life unnoticed.

Was it that formidable woman who told you about Ellen's
illness? You think that you spied me at NK. I am not at all sure
when it comes to you. But I have a very clear impression of an

elegant wide-brimmed hat and an amused glance underneath it. Was it you who sat together with a little grey mouse of a woman and looked at me? I never imagined you would be wearing such a dramatic hat. I am easily frightened and I fled helter-skelter.

I didn't have much time to dwell on our disappointing meeting, because early the next morning I found Ellen lying on the floor of her bedroom. The paramedic team went into action when I summoned them. I had never imagined they would take so much time and trouble over such an old person. It was impressive. You probably also know 'by chance' what the diagnosis is; it has been officially established that there is something wrong with her thyroid gland. She is already on the way to recovery and has been sent to a convalescent home. The prognosis seems to be good. One just hopes that it is correct. It is difficult to know what is illness and what is the natural effect of old age when it comes to a person as old as Ellen. Death has often been on my mind these days.

By the way, did you know that the blood is pumped through the heart and then runs through the body's arteries with greater force than when one turns on a water tap to its fullest extent. That's if I have understood it correctly. It sounds amazing. For an old historian it is not easy to understand the forces which drive our hearts and thereby the whole of our existence. Perhaps I should enrol myself on a biology course for pensioners – but that isn't going to happen.

Dear Anna, my behaviour at NK was cowardly and unforgiveable. But, anyway, what do you think? Shall we spit on our palms and try again? Now that we know a little more about each other and our weaknesses.

On reading through this letter I discovered an allusion to Winnie the Pooh that could perhaps be misunderstood. If I remember correctly, Pooh dates from the 1950's,[23] and it was a little pretentious of me to quote him. I never saw the book as a child but read it out loud for my daughters as a bedtime story. We all loved it. At Christmas when I wanted to read it to the grandchildren it became apparent that they had already heard everything in the kindergarten and playground and had their own tape and cassettes and preferred a shortened version. I was childishly disappointed. That is the reason why Piglet was haunting my thoughts.

Actually, it feels good to have been unmasked. Now at least we can stop creeping around.

Affectionately

Bo

★

Anna's answer took a while to arrive. That wasn't something that bothered him. He just noticed it. The ball was in her court and it was up to her to set the pace.

The dizzying happiness he had felt when Ellen began to revive again and smile at him with life in her eyes began to fade a little. Obviously he was glad that she was alive but still, he sometimes wondered if it would not have been better if she had died when he was prepared for it. Then it would all have been safely over. Now, sooner or later, it would happen again. He wondered if his daughters were thinking the same thing with regard to him: hoping that he would die before he gave them a permanently bad conscience and was a babbling burden to be looked after.

If so, they had every right to feel that way.

Ellen must have sensed the nearness of death. He couldn't believe anything else. But she'd said nothing about it, just as throughout her life she had refused to concern herself with disagreeable things. If she was worried about the future then she was concealing it. He was angry with her – but relieved at the same time – that she refused to talk about the big problems piling up in front of them. Would she be able to go on living in her apartment? Would she be able to manage on her own? She seemed wholly uninterested in speaking to a counsellor. So long as she stayed in rehabilitation in Sköndal she was satisfied. She dismissed his anxious questions with the response 'things would sort themselves out in time.'

Perhaps she thought that she would die all of a sudden before anything more needed to be done. She was not afraid and took up her old routine again, wanted to have visitors, liked small gifts of fruit, confectionery and detective novels. She was wearing her own clothes and had taken a taxi to the hairdresser. And naturally she began to put on her usual make-up even though it was applied a bit unevenly. Her ancient cavaliers came tottering in to cheer her up, an autumnal gathering shedding their leaves in a ring around her. He felt almost young when he saw them.

One frosty winter day Bo shook himself free of everything that had to do with illness and sat down in his car. For company he had Nisse who actually belonged to Karin's family but who from time to time was shunted over to him. Karin gave many reasons why she didn't have time for the dog which she'd previously claimed always to have wanted. Bo was happy to help her with him and gratified to notice that Nisse was pleased to be with him too. Perhaps it was more restful than at Karin's where it seemed no one ever had time to sit still.

What he disliked most was that they were usually standing in the kitchen as if under a time limit before the next item on the programme. He did not understand all that rushing about – riding, gymnastics, ballet, swimming. Did every minute have to be filled with some activity. Was it so wrong to sit at the table in peace and quiet in your own home?

Marianne didn't like dogs. Although she'd resembled the healthy daughter of a country mansion who should have been surrounded by dachshunds and hunting dogs from birth, the only animal she'd ever showed any interest in was Sofia's plump pony. There was a very smiley photograph of her demonstrating that. She was standing close to Sofia's pointed jodhpur-clad knee, out of reach of any possible biting or kicking. Her hand was resting lightly on the pony's withers and Sofia was smiling patronisingly at her grandmother from her superior position in the saddle.

Nisse was not yet a part of the family when this photo was taken. Marianne had warned Karin emphatically against getting a dog, saying she had more than enough to do with work and the children. He knew Marianne herself wouldn't have liked it.

But Bo became fond of the dog from the first moment and would happily have borrowed him for longer periods, but Karin always maintained that the children would miss him. Bo wasn't so sure about that. There were always plenty of excuses from them when Nisse needed to be taken out in the morning and evening. And he could understand that. He too had found it difficult at first to get used to the evil smelling heaps which Nisse deposited and which he then had to manoeuvre into a black bag and then empty into a dog latrine. Size was Nisse's only fault. Obviously a small dog would have produced less.

Apart from that practical problem, Bo felt that his enjoyment of life was increased when he had Nisse with him. Naturally there were some anxious moments. Irish Setters like to run for miles and Nisse was no exception. It often took a while before he came back, with his tongue hanging out and flecks of foam over his nose and chest. And while Nisse was amiability itself, he became very excited when he met other canines. Bo had no desire to risk life and limb in a dog fight. Nor did he want to get into arguments with angry landowners, cat owners or irritated owners of fleeing bitches.

The best way of avoiding such incidents was to drive out to the country with Nisse on the back seat. They had taken long walks together in Lovön and Svartsjö and Bo was always pleased to see Nisse running free. He, who had never had anything to do with animals, had found a companion. Now they were on their way to a new destination just outside Båsla. Anna's postcode covered a large area but he had ringed a location on the map using the information she had given him: the view over the lake from the kitchen and the glimpse of the church. He knew more or less where he and Nisse should look for the Ljungs' house.

Nisse had woken up and was panting into Bo's neck with anticipation Then he sighed and laid his large heavy head on Bo's shoulder. He leaned his chin on Nisse's warm cheek. Their closeness filled him with a feeling of warmth and security.

It had been many years since he had explored Mälaren's small churches and their treasures. His intention had been to put the material into a three-part report. It was never written; instead he was called up to guard the country's borders. But he still remembered how he had cycled from one church to another with his things packed in his bicycle-bag and a wonderful feeling of freedom in his heart. He knew Anna's local church well. Among the tenant farmers close by had lived a girl with dark eyes and an unusual first name which he had long-since forgotten. She milked the cows morning and evening and in between drove the horse-rake; in the autumn she would leave to study law in Uppsala. He helped with the haymaking because there was a shortage of men. Her hair smelled faintly of cow and fresh milk and she treated lovemaking as the most natural thing in the world. She was called Torun. Her name suddenly came into his head. He was happy to remember her.

The little church lay just outside the village at a crossroads. The door stood ajar and he couldn't resist looking in. Inside there was an exquisite carving of a man's head and a sculpture of the Virgin Mary in all her innocence from the fifteenth century. He would like to take a look at them again.

A woman in a dark-green quilted jacket on top of an overall and long trousers was vacuuming the carpet in front of the altar and for a moment he thought that it might be Anna. The age was about right. But Anna had never suggested that in addition to translating she also cleaned churches. She didn't seem to be interested in religion but, after all, what she had revealed of herself was probably only the tip of the iceberg. She hadn't given much hint of the dark night of the soul.

The memory of Torun and seeing the carved head again made Bo feel talkative. He spoke a bit to the cleaner when she had finished the vacuuming. He had never found it difficult to talk to people, perhaps because he was naturally curious. For a moment he was tempted to ask where the Ljungs lived, but didn't think that would be fair and resisted the temptation. Anyway, the woman appeared to be in a hurry. It seemed a funeral was about to take place.

If Håkan had died, then that would explain why Anna hadn't answered his letter and everything would be so much simpler. Håkan's dumb presence disturbed him, though he knew it couldn't be helped. But something told him that Anna's husband was still above ground.

He left the car at the parking lot in the village after he had taken another look at the map. Then he followed the narrow gravel path down to the lake while Nisse roamed over the adjacent fields. It was an ordinary landscape with oak-tree covered hills and hawthorn hedges. Everything seemed to be sunk in a slumber. He saw horses standing dreaming in the pastures and jostling each other outside their stable, but he didn't see any people. There wasn't even a tractor roaring in the distance and no electric saw could be heard from the woods. Perhaps they were all working in the town. He didn't know much about life in the country.

The sun was low and the shadows long. Rime was lying on the thickets and paths and glittered on last year's grass. Nisse chased pheasants among the blackthorn and hawthorn bushes. His tail was high in the air as he gave chase and the birds broke out and flew over the ground into a new thicket. But that didn't worry Bo. Birds had wings. Nisse couldn't do any real harm. But he didn't feel relaxed. Since he was now in Anna's neighbourhood it was quite possible that she would appear. If she were alone then it would be a relief to go forward and introduce himself. Here on the open road he couldn't mistake her identity. He felt sure about that. There weren't exactly many people around to choose from. But he didn't think she would go far without her husband and dog and that would mean their meeting would be more risky. In order to be secure on this occasion he should have put on an old dark blue windcheater, a dark blue cap, a pair of thick grey trousers and tractor sole shoes. And he had Nisse with him – that was his real trump-card because he hadn't written a line to her about Nisse. And a dog gave a person a right to walk on country roads without causing any concern.

He whistled to Nisse because they were already down by the lake and the path curved down directly to the water. The shiny dark water gleamed among the clumps of reeds and he was afraid that Nisse would go too far out on the thin ice at the edge and fall through. It would be best to go up into the wood and avoid all danger of a possible meeting on the path.

It was a mossy wood of thin spruce trees. There should be some chanterelle mushrooms there. Marianne had taught him how to be an excellent mushroom-picker. In her family mushroom-picking was almost an addiction. He also had a distinct recollection that Anna had never mentioned mushrooms and it struck him that a mushroom-picking walk would have been something to talk about at the beginning. One had company on mushroom-picking walks, but not too close, and attention was focussed on the ground and not each other. While people were searching they had time to get used to one another.

But now it was the wrong time of year. And even if it had been the right time Håkan would have been trudging behind, silent and enigmatic. Bo could not free himself from the thought and another association came to him, a line of English poetry that had recently been on his mind: 'But at my back I always hear, time's wingèd chariot hurrying near.'

So there it was. He and Anna didn't have so much time and the possible happiness they could get from one other was wholly dependent upon a man for whom Bo could not help but feel a certain sympathy. There had been times in his own life when he was ashamed to admit that he would have liked to have stayed silent when faced with Marianne's never-ending chatter. But obviously he hadn't dared to take the kind of evasive action Håkan did.

He followed an animal trail through the wood and came back to the gravel path. Nisse seemed to have got over his manic bursts of enthusiasm and kept close. They went on further and came upon a long row of post-boxes that had been set up facing a farm track. This was obviously a small summer house area with yellow post-boxes announcing that the post would be collected at the latest at 18.00 on weekdays and at 13.30 on Sundays. The summer houses crouched shyly behind their leafy hedges. Green plastic dustbins were prominently placed at each entrance. He carefully read all the names on the post-boxes but it was dull reading – just the name, post-box number and post-code. The old farm and cottage names had vanished under the post-office tyranny. It didn't help if people painted birds or flowers on the boxes – the country was poorer for having been robbed of its history.

He went further and then there was a signboard that told him that he was on Enskild Road. That made him a little thoughtful, as if Anna owned the road and had set up an invisible barrier. Now that he had passed the summer-house area in the woods the landscape opened up again into pastures down by the lake and open fields inland. He had thought that her house would be somewhere in that area but he would obviously have to go up the hill to be able to see it. He would just confirm that it was there but he would not go closer and definitely not check for her name on the post-boxes he found.

With his hands clasped behind his back he strode on up the hill, pleased to notice how fit he was. He did not hear the car coming up behind him until it was quite close. Then he quickly stepped to the side and whistled to Nisse who was sauntering along slightly in front of him. Nisse turned around and trotted back then stood in the middle of the road in front of the car with his tail wagging as usual. Bo had to pull him aside by his collar and gave a little wave of apology to the windscreen for the dog's behaviour. Half blinded by the sun, he glimpsed an elderly pair in the darkness behind the windscreen, the man at the wheel and the woman beside him. The man raised his hand in acknowledgement barely a centimetre above the wheel and drove past.

Bo was suddenly positive that the woman had been Anna although he hadn't gathered anything about her other than that she was female. He forced himself to walk on as calmly as he could for as long as he could be seen in the rear-view mirror. It didn't take many seconds before the car disappeared over the brow of the hill. All he saw, strictly speaking, was a dark blue Volvo of the type that seemed to be able to survive rough farm roads for any length of time.

There was no reason to think that Anna had recognised him. She could only have seen his back when he pulled Nisse aside, possibly had a glimpse of his face. Nisse must have taken all of her attention when he stood there unblinking, with his tail wagging hopefully.

Bo stood next to the old oak tree just below the top of the hill. A farm lay right at the end of the road. Then there was just an old tractor path through the wood to the promontory. The terrain before him corresponded to the map he'd consulted. But the house was more beautiful and more well-maintained than he had expected. A short tree-lined avenue led up to the forecourt and the orchard was full of low, well-pruned fruit trees. The Volvo stood on the paved area with its doors open. The man was already on his way into the house, a carrier bag in each hand. They looked heavy. From that distance he appeared pleasant and helpful. Bo hadn't thought of Håkan as being like that. In his imagination Håkan sat silent and upright in an armchair in front of the window. From that position he would watch movement in and out with an unchanging expression on his face. But that helpful chap who trotted along with carrier bags didn't accord with this image. Bo felt a bit cheated.

Then a little dog shot out of the entrance hall like a rocket and frightened a flock of crows off the lawn as he rushed up to the car. The woman bent down for a pat. It seemed to be a tender and affectionate meeting. She was also carrying heavy bags and moved rather rigidly, as if the burden were making her stiff. Bo wished that he had a pair of binoculars. She either had a white hat on her head or her hair was shining in the low sun. She was wearing a kind of dark jacket or coat over dark trousers. It was impossible to know whether this was the same woman who had worn that dashing hat. He couldn't make out exactly what she looked like but he knew this must be Anna.

She was definitely not a young girl but struggled heavily laden towards the house at the speed of an elderly person. To Bo's surprise the discovery filled him with affection. He leaned against the oak tree and followed her with his eyes. But he was an uninvited guest on the Ljungs' territory and he needed to leave before someone discovered him. The only thing he could do was to turn back although he was very tired now and felt suddenly dejected. Common sense had caught up with him. He had been foolish again, really puerile. The only comfort was that he didn't think she had recognised him. Nonetheless he listened anxiously for the sound of a car coming up behind him.

He wasn't overtaken and he didn't meet any more cars. Still he didn't feel secure until he and Nisse were sitting in his own vehicle and on their way home.

★

The man with the Red Setter didn't seem to hear their car. He walked on unperturbed in the middle of the road with his hands clasped behind his back. She could never understand how men found that comfortable but Håkan often walked like that and her father did the same. A dog lead hung down from his gloved hands like a long rat's tail.

It wasn't anyone she knew, no one from hereabouts. They would take a tractor or a car if they wanted to go anywhere, but not in the middle of the day. The dog was also unrecognisable. There were Border-Collies, Labradors and Sheep-dogs in the district, and also Dachshunds but no Irish Setters. She looked at the man suspiciously. There was certainly something vaguely familiar about his back and shoulders.

Only when they drew nearer did the man notice the car and move to the side. But the dog stood in front of them in the middle of the road.

'Not much control over that Setter,' she said and felt Håkan's silent agreement. 'But it's a beautiful dog anyway.'

The man grabbed it by the collar and pulled it to the

verge. He smiled apologetically at the windscreen. She was sure that he had only a very limited view of her and Håkan but she could see him clearly and immediately recognised him although she usually had a bad memory for faces. There he stood, her old archivist, screwing up his eyes against the sun, a little embarrassed and in a different get-up from last time – plus the dog. But that didn't take her in. At first she felt a little amused, almost flattered. Just to think that he was so interested! Then she felt annoyed. What did he think he was doing? Was he spying on her? Did he want to find out her social status and whether she was worth troubling himself for? It was not by pure chance that he found himself in that narrow, out of the way road, she was sure.

The encounter had disturbed Håkan. It didn't take much to put him in a bad mood. Perhaps he was thinking that the man with the Setter was looking for a place to burgle. Be that as it may, once back in the house he was soon standing at the window and surveying the area through binoculars.

'Is he still there?' she asked.

But obviously he wasn't because Håkan put down the binoculars. And he was clearly annoyed that she was going to the funeral. He might be silent but his body language was clear.

On the way to the church she wondered if she would overtake Bo and if in that case she should stop. But both he and the dog had disappeared into thin air. She couldn't believe they could have left the area so quickly.

It annoyed her that she was rushing to the church with her head full of all the wrong kind of thoughts. She should have been thinking about Hilding. He had been a good neighbour for many years. She felt ashamed when she thought how one-sided that neighbourliness had been. He had brought over wood and manure for them, he had even come and towed the car when it wouldn't start and was generally there to help with all the little catastrophes. In addition his sheep and cows had kept their pastures free from brushwood. She had never managed to give him any money, but was always happy to put a cup of coffee for him on the kitchen table. She would miss him – his slow movements, his rumbling voice and obscure jokes. All the time he had probably been thinking that she and Håkan were really helpless.

'How is it with the old man,' he would ask. 'Has he said anything?' Perhaps he had meant it as a joke.

'It's tricky, this business of silence,' he had said only about a month ago. He was childishly amused by Håkan's little character quirk. Still the silence was never aimed at him. Håkan answered when Hilding spoke to him.

And now there was one less person to be puzzled by her husband's peculiarities. That was no consolation. It had been a long time since she had been worried by what people said about her and Håkan. There were others hereabouts who were also peculiar. Stina from Yellow Cottage never went out during the winter months, even though she was perfectly mobile and only fifty years old. And Sixten who lived in Änga was a pensioner who spent his time catching rats in cages and then releasing them just outside the garden fence.

She slipped into the church among the very last comers and sat down on one of the benches at the back. Suddenly she missed Håkan. It would have felt better to be here as a couple. Obviously he didn't go to funerals. But for her the village community meant something, however much of an outcast she was. She lived her odd life with her odd man and her odd job

100

and couldn't afford to cut off even the most tenuous connection to the people around her. And she had liked Hilding.

She had only a slight acquaintance with his family. His wife suffered a lot from rheumatism and none of the boys wanted to take over the farm. It would have to be sold. That was sad but the saddest thing of all was that Hilding had been a strong and healthy man. Everyone wondered why the tractor dragged him round the sand pit and battered him to death. It would probably be a long time before people stopped speculating about it.

There was a heavy atmosphere in the church. Death had come unexpectedly this time and it was frightening. 'One is never more than a heartbeat away from the end,' whispered someone in the front row. Anna sat still, looked serious and stared straight ahead, but she wasn't thinking about Hilding. Instead she saw Bo walking in front of her with the Red Setter. Then she felt ashamed. She should have been able to focus on the seriousness of life during the brief service.

At the end of the proceedings it became particularly difficult. The widow and the eldest boy went up to the coffin. The priest stepped to one side and put a supportive arm around the mother. He stopped again on the steps to make sure that the son didn't move too quickly and disturb the ceremony. He was a good priest. Anna liked him even though she didn't go to church and had never heard him preach. But she knew that he was kind to the older people and cared about his flock. He took notice of what was going on in the countryside and could distinguish between the four types of grain. He didn't want to introduce new ways of doing things and kept to the well-known hymns. The fact that the singing sounded thin was not his fault.

Leaving the church without paying respects to Hilding in his coffin would not have looked good. But it would take time. The church was almost full. While she waited for her turn she wondered how many people would have come if it had been her or Håkan lying there. Perhaps twenty, if she counted some rather unattractive people who had married second cousins. Then she thought of Gertrud and her old classmates. Perhaps there would be thirty, if they took the train and then shared a taxi from the station. But there would not be many. She couldn't expect that. It said something about her unsatisfactory life. But funerals had the advantage that the principal person involved wouldn't be worried about the attendance. It wasn't like a fiftieth birthday party. One was too embarrassed not to go to that. But Håkan didn't think it was so stupid, all things being considered. In some ways he had been mature for longer than she had — he wasn't bothered by other people's opinions. And he didn't have any religious beliefs. She herself would like to see a sign that she had meant something to someone or had done something meaningful — even if was just a really good translation.

And the children — she could only speculate about how they would react to her death. But children inevitably lose their parents and there is nothing so tragic about that. It was how life was. She could imagine that in the sadness of the moment they would talk to each other about what a pity it was that they had never really got to know their mother or father. As if it didn't count that they had spent their childhood and youth living with them. It wouldn't even occur to them that her constant letters and phone calls were an attempt to keep the dialogue between them alive.

She also wondered what – if anything – they would want

to keep of the old home. There was a chest of drawers she was attached to. It would be sad if it ended up on the rubbish tip. They would certainly look after the silver and porcelain. But the books – alas the books that had been so carefully collected – they would be sold by the yard to an auction house. And all the papers, letters and photographs which might possibly have thrown some light on her and Håkan's personalities would be burned on a big bonfire in the garden. And then there would be no trace of what they'd never bothered to find out while the parents were still alive.

It was all so sad. And when, finally, she moved forward as almost the last person to go past the pews and up to the coffin, she was tearful and had to get out her handkerchief.

'Hello Hilding, and thank you,' she thought, and laid her rose at the foot of the coffin. She couldn't think of any better farewell than that. Then she curtseyed. But on the way back to her seat she could only think what they would say at coffee. 'Imagine Anna Ljung taking it so badly! Who would have thought it? But it's understandable. How would they have managed without Hilding?'

She didn't stay for the memorial service in the church hall but drove straight home. And then something strange happened – Håkan spoke to her.

'Well, how was it?' he asked.

Because she knew that he perceived her outing as an example of herd mentality she did not answer.

But in the middle of the night she woke up and wondered if he had tried to reach out to her; if he had had something else, something more important to say and if she had passed up the opportunity to hear it. In the darkness she tried to hear whether he was awake or not. They each lay in their own room with the doors open to the hall so that Fabian could change his sleeping place if he wanted to. Perhaps also for security reasons. If something dreadful happened, either of them could hear and call for help.

She was so accustomed to interpreting his silence that she could almost with certainty determine whether he was awake or not. But he slept quietly and sometimes she imagined that he had stopped breathing. It was a long time since she had padded across the hall to listen at his doorway. But she was doing that now. And he was definitely asleep.

She groped her way back to her own bed and discovered that Fabian had had the cheek to move up from the foot of the bed to the cosy warmth of the pillow. He smelled like a clean young dog and his breath came in small warm puffs against her neck when she pulled the eiderdown over them both. But she couldn't sleep. She thought about Gertrud who had shared a double bed with Bengt so long as he was alive. How difficult she had found it to get used to sleeping alone. The feeling of security had vanished, she said. No one stroked her cheek any more.

The memory of that feeling of security made Anna envy her. Then she thought of Hilding in his coffin and his poor wife in her lonely bed. And then of her old archivist with the Setter. Nothing all around her but lonely people.

Bo!

Oh, you sly old dog! 'Let's end the sneaking around,' you said. But what do you call your visit here then? And so smart – with a Setter! I had thought of you as a man who couldn't be bothered with dogs and cats. Not that there's anything wrong with that.

But the business with the dog was still a mistake. If he hadn't been with you I wouldn't have looked at you twice, but I keep a check on all the dogs in the district and on their masters and mistresses. Because I couldn't place it, I looked again. And I recognised your back and your gait, because you went to and fro over the marble floor of NK so many times.

Surely you didn't think of going right up to our house and knocking on the door, did you? I entirely understand that you must be wondering about me and Håkan, but there should be some limits to curiosity. Håkan gets anxious if there are unexpected meetings and visits, even though they would not seem unnatural to anyone else. It doesn't take much to unbalance him.

He has actually been speaking to me lately. Three words even. But I don't think in the least that it was the sight of you that made him talkative. It is more likely to have something to do with the fact that a neighbour of ours has died. Something like that can be disturbing.

Now I have strayed quite far from the purpose of this letter. It was to answer your question. You certainly guessed correctly. The formidable woman at the hospital is one of my oldest friends and not particularly dangerous. But she is a *Who's Who?* aficionado of the highest order and immediately recognised your Ellen. When she was a child she lived exactly opposite you on Artillery Street and she admired Ellen immensely. She was mad about her, as we said in those days. I personally have only a vague memory of sweet Ellen. She was already going to the high school when we were in the elementary school. But we had Ingeborg Rydeman as our religion teacher some terms or years later. She was your mother, wasn't she?

My good friend has no idea that we two are writing to each other. I'm not particularly proud of the fact that I advertised for a penfriend. I don't think that any good can come of it. In the night I thought that it was altogether pathetic. I thought that it was time to say enough. But now I don't really know. Do you understand what I mean? For the moment I am fine. Work on a new book is something solid I can get my teeth into.

Anna

★

She wasn't particularly satisfied with the letter but she had got down the most important things. It was just as well that Bo knew that she was acquainted with Ingeborg Rydeman. If she had kept it secret and he had still got to know, then he might have thought that she thought that he was ashamed of her – which obviously must be precisely what he was.

'Search you heart. If you knew that you were going to die in a week's time what would weigh most heavily on your conscience? An unresolved quarrel, worry about some wrongdoing, a feeling of guilt about someone you loved or love?'

It was evening and they had just watched the news. Now the television had been switched off, the wood was crackling and the fire was giving out warmth and light. It wasn't in any way cheerless. Håkan was reading P.D. James and she was leafing through the newspaper when she came upon an article on a page of *Idag* about problem-solving skills. An ever-important subject and this time in American-Tibetan-Buddhist style, which didn't sound particularly reassuring. But perhaps there was something to be learned from it.

First you had to look into your heart. And then shut your eyes – that seemed to be important – and then think about the problem while still keeping your eyes shut. Then summon up the person one wanted to be reconciled with and begin a dialogue with him or her. The whole thing was an exercise in making a good farewell, she read. Who that was good for – the one who was going to die or the one left behind – wasn't clear.

She didn't need to summon up anyone with powerful thoughts and closed eyes. Håkan was sitting before her in his chair by the fire, so near that she could touch him with her hand. But he was still beyond her reach. That was the big betrayal, the unresolved problem. And she could never persuade him to play along with some artificial dialogue in the Tibetan-American fashion.

There was no big unresolved quarrel in their life. Not even a small one. One can't argue with someone who doesn't answer. On the other hand, one could in quarrelsome desperation pursue an inner monologue full of bitter accusations against him. But in the end it was meaningless and just caused grief.

If there was anyone she wanted to confront, it was the young Håkan with whom she had been so hopelessly in love and who was also good at jilting. The old Håkan was still a good-looking man, but he had lost the allure he'd had as a young one. With a little effort she could summon up the young Håkan from the shadows and see him in front of her. A very British type, familiar after the war. Leather patches on the elbows, a pipe in the mouth, irony and humour apparent, with a hint of superiority but also of integrity – so far but no further. And then there was his penchant for women. They didn't have to be particularly bright – intelligence and logic were his domain – they just had to be good looking. If they were already involved with someone else it meant nothing to him. Rather the opposite. Girls who were engaged or half engaged were something he couldn't resist. It was as if he had immediately to show that he could get whoever he wanted. Obviously he didn't manage it every time, but the curious thing was that in those cases it was generally the girls who were considered at fault, not him.

It was entirely predictable that he would be interested in Gertrud. She was sweet, witty and flirtatious. And besides she was 'going steady' with her Bengt who was then only a young medical student with pock-marked skin and a nervous smile, but disarmingly good-natured in all circumstances.

Gertrud enjoyed being with Håkan but she didn't take any risks. Her sense of self-preservation was functioning perfectly. Anna's was much worse. She didn't take love light-heartedly, was slow and hesitant at first, unlike Gertrud who could be excited by almost anything – a boyish neck, a dimple in the chin, Håkan's sparkling brown eyes, just about anything. But without losing control. So she decided on Bengt. His future was more secure.

Håkan's sudden interest in Anna began at the same time as Gertrud's engagement. To punish her. At least, that was what Gertrud thought and what she gave Anna to understand. She warned Anna, because what did they really know about Håkan? He was certainly good looking and clever, but not someone whose hand you could hold when it thundered.

Anna just laughed at her. For once she was in a superior position. In love and happy, almost unbelievably happy.

'But you were never actually in love with me. Not even at the beginning.'

In the subsequent silence she was amazed at her words. They had slipped out unexpectedly. Håkan looked up from his book. There was something unusual about the sound of her voice. Sometimes she spoke as if she had received a reply, and she always kept him informed about what was going on around them. If she spoke to friends on the telephone, she conveyed their greetings to him and spoke about new things that had happened to them, if there were any such.

That was happening less frequently. Sometimes he listened to her, sometimes not, and sometimes he answered her with a mutter or even a few words if he was feeling benevolent. It also sometimes happened that he laughed at something on the TV. He wasn't always enveloped in silence. People could still reach him, if they wanted to.

Now he looked at her with a little smile, not dissimilar to the smile he bestowed on Fabian. You could call it affectionate, she thought. Then he cleared his throat as he usually did before saying anything.

'I've always enjoyed being with you.'

That was all he said. A few minutes later he put his book down and got up.

She stayed sitting down, shaken by the experience. The thought came to her that perhaps he was emerging from his depression. That perhaps they could be like other people again. Though she should have known that a few words every now and then meant nothing in the bigger picture. It had happened before. If he woke up and felt like communicating that could also mean trouble. That had happened as well. But she had thought those episodes were over.

In any case she felt almost mild-tempered. Mild and tolerant, completely without resentment towards him. It was understandable, almost half a century away from the first torment of love and betrayal. The young Håkan wasn't to blame for the fact that she had fallen for him and he had done what was expected of him, almost good-naturedly, even though she insisted she could manage on her own. No one compelled him, although her family did have certain views on the matter. The most important thing was that the child would have a father who looked good and knew how to behave.

Her sisters had had bridesmaids and a church wedding. Anna was glad to get out of that. The wedding was unpretentious. Almost shameful.

But it wasn't likely that he would have married her if she hadn't been expecting a baby. When a little girl was born two months too early and died after a few days, there was no suggestion that they should separate. She was much too overcome by feelings of guilt and grief. She certainly hadn't wanted the baby to live during the first few months. Forget that and draw a line under everything, the midwife had quickly said. Don't think about the past. Just look forward and start again.

But the dead child followed her through the years. The sorrow didn't fade. Håkan got off more lightly. The child hadn't been so real for him. He hadn't formed a bond with it. But he was kind and patient with her. He behaved so well that she suspected that he thought it gave him certain rights. And that wasn't without some foundation. Without the freedom he took for himself, he probably would not have had so much patience with her.

Objectively speaking, it was obviously a bad beginning that they'd had to get married. And that it then turned out to be unnecessary. That would explain a lot. But perhaps the strangest thing was that he never really wanted a divorce. Having things both ways was his ideal and he couldn't understand why she reacted so badly to his affairs on the side. They seldom lasted for long and didn't mean anything to him. But every time she found out about one she immediately wanted a divorce but then everything ran aground. When it came to the crunch she didn't dare to do it. She wasn't sure that she would be able to manage financially on her own and

111

Nan Östman

was afraid that the children would suffer. Besides: a divorce is always a big disaster, however hard one tries to smooth it over.

She didn't play an edifying role in these disputes. He ran after women and she sulked. It was as simple as that.

But that wasn't the whole truth.

What was meant as thought play made her depressed. It was too late to bring up old grievances now. She was just as good at arguing as he was. Their children really couldn't boast that they had grown up in a loving home where they had never heard a bad word exchanged by their parents. Quite the opposite. Harsh words flew like blow-flies through the room, fat and black; doors were slammed, cars roared off and disappeared into the darkness.

No, it hadn't been an idyll for the poor children. She couldn't think about it anymore. Slowly she tore the article into pieces and put them on the glowing heap of the open fire. They burned with a clear blue flame.

They would never divorce now. They had reached some kind of reconciliation. After all his roving around the world he now lived shielded and protected from its temptations – but also without stimulation and pleasure. She was responsible for them both. She couldn't just leave. The moment had passed, but he didn't feel confident about it. He would have preferred to have her tied to a long rope in the garden so that he could hear her yapping and know where she was.

He was content with her.

★

Once again the days passed without anything happening. They lived their quiet life, each going their separate way. No one called. No one came to visit. It was as if they were cut off from the world.

During such days Anna had unreasonable expectations of the country postwoman. She not only saw her through Gullberg's[24] eyes as bringing messages from person to person, but also as a source of happy and unexpected surprises. For Håkan she was almost entirely negative – a symbol of bills, unwanted offers and ridiculous and often unintelligible notices from the authorities.

Still, he trudged out to the post box as soon as he spied the yellow van up on the bend. He seemed as impatient to receive bad news as she was to receive good, perhaps to get over the discomfort as quickly as possible. Since Bo now had her address, she was anxious not to appear too eager one morning when Håkan brought in the post but continued to dry the kitchen floor while he sorted the day's haul into two heaps, one for her and one for him. But it was unnecessary play-acting. He was not interested in whatever lay in her heap. She often received letters. An amazing number of readers saw it as their duty to inform her that she had misunderstood or mistranslated a word or expression. She could almost imagine their delight when they came across something questionable and compared the original text and the translation. Still they were usually kind and she had almost become friends with some of her most faithful critics.

Håkan held a postcard in his hand, looking puzzled. For a moment she thought that he intended to show it to her, but then he snorted softly and put it down again. Without giving her a glance he turned to open a fuel bill and what looked like a bank statement.

She poured the water out of the bucket and was astonished

as always at how much dirt two quiet people and one young dog managed to bring in onto the floor. Although that could be explained easily since neither Håkan nor Fabian was over-inclined to wipe their feet. Then she went over to the kitchen table and saw that Bo had written to her. But she didn't let on. Instead she leafed through the local council's free newspaper and came across an extensive article on dementia in the elderly. She was terrified by the illnesses of old age. And how could she be anything else when one was reminded of one's mortality every time she opened a newspaper or switched on the radio? Not to mention the television where a TV doctor appeared every week to talk about a large number of frightening illnesses. She didn't find talk of illness entertaining. It was bad enough with serious explanations. But there were some people in the media who wanted to hustle her – and countless other pensioners – prematurely into old age by constant reminders of what awaited them. There was one distressing report after another, interspersed with joyful accounts of bungee-jumping ninety-year-olds and one-hundred-year olds with sweat bands on their foreheads competing in the Vasa ski race.

When she was a child there had been a completely different style of life among old people. They didn't throw themselves off cranes with rubber bands attached to their legs. They died because they had a stroke or just faded away. If they became forgetful, it was put down to hardening of the arteries and not dementia.

'Oh, my hardened arteries,' said Anna's mother, excusing herself when she mislaid her glasses, or forgot a name. It sounded as though she was speaking about a delicate but loved child who could be forgiven for everything. Her father never referred to hardening of the arteries as a cause of his forgetfulness. But he was a man and on the whole didn't make mistakes. And in any case he died before he developed ailments.

Håkan carried on sitting with the fuel bill in front of him, looking worried, as if he couldn't rightly understand how the figure could be so high. It was a blow to him. He had always been so quick with calculations. Now everything took longer. And there was the same silence between them as always.

Would he be upset with her if he knew about her correspondence with Bo? That was difficult to believe. So long as she served as Håkan's buffer against the world, she could write to whomever she pleased. Although naturally he wouldn't understand what the purpose of it was or what she got out of it.

That was something for her to consider.

He sighed and went upstairs with his post. She listened to his footsteps on the stairs and over the hall floor. Then everything went quiet until he sat on his bed, took off his shoes and let them fall to the floor, one after the other. The thuds were the signal for Fabian to come and he got out of his basket. The two men always slept together at midday, after lunch.

She looked at the postcard he had left on the table. It was written in English and the writing was very cramped and difficult to read. Someone had met someone at a conference and both sent [in English] their 'best wishes and hope to meet'. She didn't bother to try and decipher the lines she couldn't make out, but just noticed that it was signed by Mary and Hilde. She turned it over. The picture was of Frankfurt and the stamp was a German one. '*Ack*, Håkan and his women.'

With a clear conscience, she took Bo's letter into her study.

Dear Anna,

I thought about a lot of things while I was out walking with my daughter's Irish setter. But as you probably noticed, I didn't have him entirely under control and that distracted me. Among the things I thought about was memory, particularly why certain childhood memories don't leave a lasting impression. The first really clear memory I have of my foster home is the long row of ski-boots in the entrance hall and the slush on the floor. It is a positive memory connected to a feeling of being lifted up in both the literal and metaphorical sense. Someone lifted me up in the air from behind and I had what was in itself a very prosaic view over the ski-boots, floating over them like a bird, while yet feeling incredibly happy.

That is not in itself particularly interesting. But why do I have no early memories of my mother? As an adult one thinks that it must be a significant event to be visited by one's real mother. And I know that she visited me at Älvsjö. But I don't remember it. Perhaps a child doesn't think that a biological mother is particularly significant. Perhaps my foster-parents had already given me a sort of basic security, so that she didn't play a large role. Unfortunately I also remember very little about my foster-parents, except that they were nice. Perhaps my memory has always been poor.

Later in life I tried to imprint particularly happy moments on my memory so that I would be able to recall them. I can remember that I thought, 'This is a happy moment, I won't forget this.' But moments of bliss don't come back again, at least not on demand.

Shame and guilt on the other hand remain fresh in the mind. They don't fade as the decades roll by. The skeleton in the cupboard was obviously my mother. As you well know she didn't exactly equate to the ideal of motherhood. I was often ashamed of her. Unfortunately she died before I was mature enough to see her with tolerance and gratitude. But my home and my growing up were probably a little strange and coming home must have been a shock. After the security of Älvsjö I found myself at the age of six in a large and dark apartment, occupied by three middle-aged women (including my mother) a rebellious and wild teenager and a terrifying housemaid. That obviously didn't last long. I was sent to Lundsberg.[25] It was certainly a good thing that I was no longer confined and became a boy among boys in an almost exclusively male world. There were enough women during the holidays.

My wife Marianne, who was over-sensitive to every form of snobbery, never stopped being surprised at Mama's choice of school and thought that it was a disastrous mistake. She blamed Lundsberg for the fact that as a boy I was afraid of standing out and hardly dared to have an opinion and stand up for it. At all cost I wanted to be like all the others. They were seen as the privileged few, though many as it happened had equally troubled backgrounds to mine though not in the same way.

And it is true that I was afraid to take a stand and avoided scenes and quarrels. But now I dare to stand by my opinion even when it is uncomfortable. Perhaps I have Marianne to thank for that.

Enough remembering. My childhood and youth are not something which I go on about every day. It is something that I accept. At least that's what I thought. I was convinced that nothing in the past could hurt me anymore. That I was invulnerable in that respect.

But I was wrong. The knowledge that you had my mother as a teacher served to let loose a host of demons that had been imprisoned in my soul. They affected me badly. Even in one's older days one is clearly thin-skinned and vulnerable. There are memories that are painful, perhaps because they are mixed with guilt. I wasn't much joy or support to my mother. I didn't want to be burdened with her problems. I just didn't want to know about them. I had enough of my own.

I hadn't intended to write that but now I have done it. What I had intended to write was an explanation of why I was strolling along your road. Naturally I was curious about where you lived but I didn't intend to make a social evaluation. I just wanted to make sure that you had a beautiful setting. You definitely have that and it fitted my picture of you. I don't agree that I was guilty of some kind of intrusion, just the usual human clumsiness. I am deeply sorry if I in some way disturbed your husband's equilibrium. I didn't expect to meet you. I still feel crestfallen at being caught in the act.

I have begged forgiveness as sincerely as I can.

By the way, I am feeling satisfied with life. I have been invited to work jointly on a paper which among other things will consider the role of the Court of Appeal in the so-called judicial revolution. A lot of new things have emerged in that area. Just like you with your work, I longed to get my teeth into something substantial. It will be good to have some structure to my days again. There has been too much running to the hospital and that isn't edifying. But Ellen should soon be home once more.

I hope that you will write to your humble friend again.

Bo

★

After a few weeks of bare ground it was proper winter again with snow, grey skies and an icy east wind. The weather wasn't inviting, but Fabian demanded his walk and Håkan and Anna plodded slowly along the road towards the forest. Fabian was frisky.

It was easier when they were properly in the forest. Håkan went in front, Anna walked behind. He was steady on his feet and rarely missed his footing. It was difficult to follow in his tracks and he was completely unconcerned about her. It didn't occur to him to turn his head to see if she was managing. Sometimes she wondered if he would have noticed if she had collapsed and died behind him. Not that she was worried about it but it would have been interesting to know.

She walked with her gaze fixed on the snow-covered ruts of the path, but in her thoughts as was so often the case, she carried on a conversation with Bo. She should answer his letter but it would be difficult and sensitive. She couldn't just write, 'Stop it, Bo! No one is responsible for their parents and stop talking about your dead wife. It seems that she could really pinch, by the way!'

He had a confidential way of writing, Bo. As if he took it for granted that she would understand.

Anna raised her eyes from the ground and fixed them on Håkan's back. He was someone who wanted neither to receive nor to share confidences. He kept his own to himself and other people's didn't interest him. The less he said about himself the better. No need to give anything away.

But that didn't mean that he wasn't moved by other people's foolishness, audacity or cowardice. He had listened to many long stories about such things; listened, agreed and supported as much as he could. But those times were long gone.

She had also discovered that it was easy to talk to Bo about Håkan. Things that she had never confided to anyone else flooded out of her during these silent one-sided conversations during long walks with the dog. But he didn't get any bedroom details. That was private and it was unthinkable she would divulge them to anyone.

Håkan's personality, on the other hand, didn't really count. At least not when one was walking in the forest. She didn't hesitate to open it up and lay it out for inspection. Bo would understand – he had his own shame and skeletons in the cupboard. But Håkan had a whole cupboard full! No wonder he had put padlocks on it so that the secrets didn't slip out. That was no longer of any importance now but when they were young and he had just established his lifelong lie, it was essential to keep such things quiet. She thought that in his insecurity he had overestimated her background. She was not at all as 'fine' as he imagined, after he had been led through the inherited (and very uncomfortable) furniture in Östermalm Street to be vetted by her parents. He probably hoped that there was money behind them – there was some but not much. Perhaps it had made her a little more attractive as a marriage prospect but all that was in the past. And he had never complained about his mistake. One had to give him credit for that, she said to Bo.

Håkan did not reveal more about himself and his upbringing other than that he had grown up in an English colony in Africa and that his parents had died out there. He gave his slightly ironic smile and gracefully fended off further questions. But sometimes he hinted at something dark and she suspected catastrophe and black secrets. Terrible things must have happened during his childhood on the plantation.

Yet there was also something alluring about the thought of such a childhood. There was something of an upper-class style about it, like Karen Blixen's African farm: silent bare-footed black servants, lions and hunting, celebrations and drums in the distance, tropical fruits and the cruel ending of all that with his parents' death. Håkan had no siblings or close relatives.

And all the while her own childhood had flowed by, dull and uneventful in grey Östermalm. The same Östermalm that Bo had moved to. They must have met as children, run past each other without leaving any impression.

To put it bluntly, though, Håkan told outright lies about his childhood and obviously he'd had to come clean about certain facts before they got married. If her parents were shocked it hardly showed. He hadn't changed much about the facts, just presented them in a different light. The missionary station became a coffee plantation, the missionaries plantation owners, and his fairly simple boarding school was miles away from an English public school. However, his English was perfect. Although he was in fact a Swedish missionary's son he could have passed for an upper-class English boy. He cultivated that image of himself. He still did that sometimes, she confided to Bo. And it impressed people.

But all that was trifling. The fact was that his parents had died in a horrible way, killed by their own black protégés and servants during an uprising. Håkan was at school and so escaped the blood-bath. She could understand why he'd kept quiet about the massacre and preferred to say that his parents died in a tropical epidemic. That didn't elicit a troubled silence, just sympathy.

People had invented worse histories than that and escaped their background. It wasn't anything to get excited about. And once the basic facts have been improved upon a little gilding often follows. It's only human.

But the worst thing of all was that there was a hint of the comic about the catastrophe for our generation, she mentally reminded Bo. As children we saw cartoons of missionaries and black people in the newspapers and laughed at them. There was one in particular that showed a white man being cooked in a pot, with just his head sticking out in a cloud of steam, while the black people stoked up the fire for all they were worth with greedy smiles on their thick lips. We thought that was just great, because we didn't know that it was wrong to laugh at black Africans. We also laughed a bit at busybody missionaries as well, who rushed off to convert the heathens and put decent clothes on them. Certainly their work was well-intentioned and self-sacrificing but they were not the ideal parents to be associated with.

Obviously it looks bad that anyone should want to disassociate themselves from their origins to disguise their social class. I believe that nowadays it is unthinkable. And our children know the truth though only in bare outline, a skeleton without flesh on the bones. Malin thought it was exciting that her father had grown up in darkest Africa, but she couldn't get any juicy stories out of him.

At that point Anna had to pause in her monologue because Håkan was climbing nimbly over a half broken-down fence while she got her foot caught in some barbed-wire. It took her a moment before she could get free and continue on the walk. By then she had lost the thread.

Anyway, Håkan was sent home to Sweden and looked after by colleagues of his parents. His schooling and further education were paid for. He developed an aversion to the whole group. Felt he was too much under their control. He responded by becoming as much of an atheist as he could. And if you think that I am going to overwhelm you with these stories you are wrong, dear Bo. There is a kind of fateful irony there. Håkan would have felt very much at home at your fine school, while you would probably have tolerated being cared for by missionaries better than he did.

Later in the day, when Håkan and Fabian had dragged themselves back for an hour's well-deserved rest, she wrote to Bo.

★

Dear Bo,

I read your letter several times, but I can't compose a sensible answer although I have really tried.

When I was young I was convinced that old people acquired wisdom and calm with the passing years; that they sat peacefully on their sofas and remembered the days gone by with sadness and gratitude. My mother wasn't exactly the picture of peaceful old-age, but I thought she was an exception. Now I know that she wasn't. An old person is the same as they always were with all the same faults plus some new ones. For example, I continue to hope that something will happen – like Nora in *A Doll's House* but obviously not so spiritualised. I am a realist to that extent.

To cut a long story short, I would like to meet you, but at the moment I can't decide when or where. But something will probably work out. I think of you very often when I do my jobs around the house. And not without affection.

Anna

The days went by. It slowly began to get lighter and one morning, in the middle of February, the great tits were singing loudly in the tall laburnums – lively and relentless. Blue tits tinkled along like small bells and their pale blue crowns had begun to darken. Flocks of greenfinches landed in the lilac tree, found the bird table and snatched up the food with hysterical flapping of their wings.

Anna and Håkan smiled when they sat down with their morning coffee and gazed at them through the kitchen window. They had become friends to small birds. Who would have believed it when they were young intellectuals and had 'views' on most things? But looking at birds through a window was an excellent occupation for those who had turned the flame down low. Håkan conscientiously took care of the provision of seeds and tallow-balls.

It was a beautiful winter morning, cold and sparkling, but later in the day there would certainly be a thaw. Snow began to drip from the gutter above the kitchen window.

'Praise be God who causes us to wake up in gladness and another day of grace to rise …' The hymn rang in Anna's head as she took Fabian out, saw him go to the lime tree and nimbly and precisely lift up his left hind leg. She couldn't get the hymn

out of her head. She had her school years to thank for that –
morning prayers for six days a week, year in year out. One
hymn before the homily and one after. It wasn't surprising that
disconnected and often truncated verses surfaced on suitable
and unsuitable occasions. It was a linguistic legacy which one
acquired in the girls' school hall while one's thoughts were
busy with other things – daydreams, injustices, lessons and
infatuations. Her children and grandchildren had missed
out on that. It seemed that she hadn't been able to pass on to
her children anything of the deep-seated pleasure she felt in
the words and rhymes, a treasure house of them for times of
need, full of faith and doomsday warnings. Her own children
had grown up in a home without faith. The missionaries'
son didn't encourage any reliance on the Christian faith. She
herself still had residual faith in the power of bedtime prayer,
almost on the sly because her parents didn't believe in what
was habitually said with folded hands after the goodnight hug
and tucking in.

While she waited for Fabian to finish his business, she
wondered, as she had often done before whether it was such a
good idea to distance oneself from the security of the Church,
from all that cultural heritage. Perhaps life would have been
different if the whole family had walked hand in hand to the
early-morning Christmas service. Or at least have gone to
church on the first day of Advent to imbibe a little holiness
and something of the Christmas spirit.

Several of her old friends took it for granted that they
would go to church from time to time and would never have
dreamed of losing that continuity. But she found it impossible
to believe. And for Håkan such a thing was inconceivable.

But on that day with its sun and cold and an unexpectedly

thick covering of snow she was more than ready to praise and thank the Heavenly Father. He deserved that.

'Perhaps we should go skiing,' she suggested.

Håkan did not respond, but his silence meant that he was thinking about it, not refusing to engage.

'Come on,' she said in the encouraging tone she used with Fabian. 'You will think it's a good idea once we're out there. We may not get many more fine days with snow.'

He wasn't markedly enthusiastic, probably because of the prospective bother of taking the skis out of the shed, undoing the straps and buckles and being obliged to confess that it was a very long time since he had stood with a blowlamp and tarred the undersides. They stayed pale year after year. A little later she saw him going to the shed looking purposeful, but also perhaps with a touch of pleasurable anticipation. He might have had an African childhood, but he was good at skiing.

It was two years since they had last been out on the snow and it felt like an adventure when they glided down to the lake: two old people in outmoded clothes, with wooden skis and boots with rat-trap bindings. For as long as she could remember Håkan had worn the same army anorak on these occasions, large and roomy with a belt around the waist, patterned with rust spots and coffee spillages on the thick woven fabric. Not even environmentally unfriendly chlorine could clean it. In the old days he had worn grey diagonally woven ski-trousers with considerable fullness in the legs; now he was wearing her rib-patterned tights under jeans. She was wearing the faded blue anorak that she had worn while expecting the two children and very old ski pants with a wide elastic strap under each foot. They didn't intend to visit tourist spots and almost no one saw them in their outfits except for two men who just happened to be out winter-fishing on the ice. She didn't know if she and Håkan would be seen as a pathetic old pair in rags or as plucky old pensioners. It was anyway unlikely that the men had even seen them. They sat on their kick-sledges and drank coffee from a thermos, watching the bore-holes, incredibly well protected from the cold by their leather hats with the flaps down.

Fabian took a quick turn around them, wagged his tail and rushed about, sniffed at the ice around the hole, stole a half-eaten sandwich from a rucksack and ran away.

Someone had been skiing before them on the slopes on the other side of the creek. The tracks wound upwards between the tufts of high yellow grass, over a ploughed field which the snow covered nice and evenly and then into the forest by a tractor path with soft foundations and an unexpectedly fine glide. There the snow was almost blue.

Suddenly Håkan came to a stop. A female moose with a year-old calf came out of the forest just a little ahead of them, crossed the track and trotted across the field into the edge of the forest on the other side. Fabian threw himself after them eagerly but fell into a ditch and crawled out somewhat subdued. He gave up for practical reasons. The snow was too deep and his legs too short.

Håkan turned around. There was colour in his cheeks and his eyes were bright. As always they both felt exhilarated by meeting the forest animals. The memory stayed with them as a shared joy.

Then he skied on at a leisurely pace. He never exerted himself more than he needed to. Nothing had ever persuaded him to jog or run just to keep himself in condition. He had never needed it. He didn't weigh any more than he had when they married. The fact that his muscles were wasting away was another matter. There wasn't much filling these days between skin and bone. He continued to enjoy seeing himself in brief bathing trunks, but the absence of paunch didn't mean that he looked like a young god. He was well on the way to becoming a skinny old man though he didn't realise it. If contrary to all expectations they were invited to a wedding, then he still invited the sweetest of the girls to dance. Anna believed he didn't realise that he was subject to the same laws of nature as everyone else.

His delusion was reinforced by the fact that he was much fitter than her. Her faults were worse and more obvious. Nothing could have induced her to sit on a beach in a bikini and expose her aging body. She could still pass when she was dressed, but she understood very well that Håkan preferred prettier women. And younger ones.

However none of that mattered any more. That was in the past. She didn't think he had the strength any longer to attempt to break away. He hadn't chased brides for a long time. But around this time of year in the past, his spirits used to revive. He'd been in the habit of going away then. She still missed those spells of undemanding solitude in the empty house. The wonderful freedom. But not now. Not today. The sun warmed their faces as they struggled up the hill. Then they would go down the other side. She was happy to have company. On her own she wasn't a bold downhill skier.

Afterwards he said, 'That was very nice.' And she was almost stunned by surprise. He stood down there on the ice with colour in his cheeks and spoke to her! The thought that perhaps he was in a better place flew through her head again. He had definitely been a little livelier recently. The other day she'd surprised him on the telephone when he thought she was otherwise occupied. He had also posted letters for her. Small steps certainly, but still a sign of increasing activity. There could be life in the old boy yet!

Halfway across the creek he stood still. 'What's that then?' he muttered. She saw the car too, a shining tomato red on their forecourt. That in itself wasn't so strange. They weren't hermits. They did sometimes have visitors. But at that moment she couldn't think of anyone they knew who had a red car.

'A Jehovah's witness?' she suggested, because they never gave up. They came back winter and summer, forever hopeful in spite of constant resistance.

He didn't answer, but she hadn't expected that he would. Instead he picked up speed. She took it for granted that he was preparing for bad news because that was his nature.

But it couldn't be the police. The car looked too red, a private vehicle. One couldn't turn up with news of a death in such a car. Also there didn't seem to be more than one person in the car. The police never arrived singly. Then she thought that it might be Bo sitting there waiting. Perhaps he had disguised himself as some kind of salesman. In the country all sorts of people visited, wanting to sell non-slip protection for steps, compost containers, fire-extinguishers and traps for badgers. She wondered what excuse Bo could come up with. He wasn't someone who could easily play a salesman.

How could she explain his visit if it really was Bo. They were already over the lake shore and up to the fence below the road. Håkan had definitely put on a burst of speed. She glanced at him sideways and was once again surprised at how lively he looked. Lively and expectant. Like a child on Christmas Eve. The door of the red car on the forecourt opened and a woman stretched out a long thin leg in a high black laced boot. Then she unfolded herself out of the car dressed in a loose black cape. One arm dressed in peacock blue emerged from it. Her tousled hair gleamed henna-red in the sunshine.

This exotic visitor felt like an intruder. She should have been laughable, dressed in such splendour on their rustic forecourt. But she wasn't.

She was alien and threatening in spite of her big smile and striking white teeth as she approached Håkan with outstretched arms and drew him to her.

He willingly allowed himself to be embraced. The man Anna had thought was out of the game. The man she thought had resigned himself to settling into old age with her.

At around lunchtime the next day Gertrud rang.

'I saw Håkan at the Opera yesterday evening with a very striking lady. Has he run away or did he have permission.'

'I gave him permission. And who were you with, may I ask?'

'Jonas obviously. We always go to the opera together. But who has Håkan got hold of? We are really curious.'

'I can believe that. She's an old friend of his, an ethnologist who specialises in the early Stone Age. She is here for a conference and had tickets for the opera.'

'Håkan has never in his life been interested in ethnology! Nor in opera so far as can I remember. But I haven't seen him looking so lively for a long time. Last Christmas he looked half dead. He was obviously getting on very well with her and she with him.'

'Yes, they enjoy each other's company,' said Anna in a casual tone.

'Stop trying to behave as though you don't care. You can't take me in. Has he run away or not?'

'I don't know whether he has run away or not. They had planned to meet at our house but she surprised us by coming a day earlier than expected. We were somewhat startled and he left in a bit of a hurry. And you know how it is. Håkan doesn't like being rushed or stressed.'

'Please, Anna, come on now. Tell me what has happened. The person didn't look like an academic but she was attractive in her way. How could you let him loose with her?'

Anna sighed. She couldn't escape from it, and maybe it was just as well. Hilde Apeldoorn must be discussed. The whole situation must be discussed. Though Gertrud was without a doubt, the last person on earth she wanted to confide in on the subject of Håkan.

'I thought she was really charming,' she protested. 'Colourful and elegant. True, Mama would have said "common" but that's not a term one should use nowadays, is it? Even if it's true. But in some ways she also seemed reliable. When she had put Håkan in the seat next to her and checked that he had done up his seatbelt, she suddenly looked to me like an old-fashioned English nanny, one of those women who doesn't stand for any nonsense. I thought that he was, after all, in safe hands.'

'You have never been much of a judge of character. An old-fashioned nanny! Where did you get that from? She looked hungry, simply ravenous. You should be pleased if she doesn't eat him up. It will be a miracle if you get him back in one piece. And how old is she then? Fifty?'

'At least fifty-five,' said Ann maliciously. 'A lot of wrinkles under the make-up.'

'But younger than us. Considerably younger than us. And nothing drooping, as far as I could see. Is she Swedish? She didn't look like it. We thought they were speaking English.'

'She's Dutch. She speaks very good English. And you know how much Håkan likes speaking English. It really brings him to life.'

'We noticed that. It looked as though they belonged to a group and she was introducing him like some kind of curiosity.'

'They were probably all at the conference.'

'Perhaps. How long do you intend to let her keep him?'

'No idea. He will stay as long as he finds it fun. Then he will most likely come back.'

The next sound on the telephone was Gertrud shaking her head vigorously in reproof.

'Have you no sense of responsibility whatsoever? Go on, admit that you have no idea what kind of person she is? Or what she knows about Håkan and his... weaknesses. Can she look after him if need be? I don't understand how you could have let him go.'

'They didn't require permission from me. It was already agreed upon. Should I really have made a scene? I also need to be alone sometimes too. Not everyone is as unencumbered as you are,' she said and then regretted it. Almost.

Gertrud snorted audibly. She was someone who really knew how to show derision.

'You should count yourself lucky for every day you live as a couple. Believe me, you have no idea what true loneliness is like. Life can feel so empty that you would be glad to hear a cough. It would be a sign of life at least.'

'You win,' said Anna. 'You definitely have it worse. But the strange thing is that we actually went skiing the morning he left with her. He spoke a little and looked so well. We had a really good time. I didn't suspect anything.'

'You never have been particularly perceptive. At least, as far as Håkan is concerned. Aren't you at all worried about him?'

Anna was silent for a long time, lost in thought. Obviously she should be worried. But she wasn't.

'I am too angry,' she said. 'One does get angry when an old man goes on a fling without any explanation, even if one has been through it before. And I think his taste in women is getting worse. She wasn't particularly good looking. But he can't expect stunners any longer. I suppose I am angry, but also relieved. At least I'll have some time to myself now. And no, I'm definitely not worried.'

'Do you even know where he is staying?'

It sounded as though Gertrud was still shocked by Anna's laidback reaction while at the same time generally excited by Håkan's escapade. Also, smugly convinced that nothing like that would have happened if she, Gertrud, had been able to keep an eye on him.

'Yes, I know the hotel where he's staying with her. She wrote down her name and telephone number in capital letters, also her home number in Holland. She promised to take good care of him.'

'Oh, come on, Anna! Didn't you think that it was strange and presumptuous of her? You don't just come sweeping in and *borrow* someone else's husband. People of our age don't behave like that. And even if she belongs to a younger one, the old buffer doesn't.'

'She didn't know we were married. It seems he's always said to her that he lived with his elder sister. God only knows if he made me out to be a widow as well. However that may be, she thought we looked very much alike.'

'Yes, marital resemblance,' retorted Gertrud. 'Don't you know about that? In the same way that people get to look like their dogs – although fortunately you and Håkan look like each other instead. All your fighting and scrapping have smoothed over the differences like constant rubbing with sandpaper. Bengt and I, who lived a different kind of life, never became similar,' she goaded. 'But never mind. If Bengt had tried to pretend that I was his elder sister, I would never have forgiven him.'

'Quite. And why should I? It was dreadful. And you know how it is now. A few years older or younger begins to be as important as when one was young. Every year makes such a difference – in the wrong direction. Then one grew bigger, stronger and more daring with the passing of every year. Now one becomes more bent, unsure and cautious. Obviously I was angry. Particularly as I'm always hearing how fit and youthful he looks. It's easy for him. He never wears himself out.'

'He does look remarkably healthy. I thought that only yesterday. Perhaps it's thanks to your very active life, skiing and running in the forest. But I don't understand how you can have failed to notice what he was planning. Do you not communicate at all?'

'We do, obviously, but we were taken by surprise. Otherwise I suppose he would have asked me to drive him to the station. But what do I know?'

'What did he have with him when he left – a big bag or a small one?'

Gertrude was relentless in her cross-examination.

'An overnight bag,' lied Anna.

She couldn't bring herself to tell the whole truth. The large suitcase was as good as already packed when she followed him up to his room to try and get some information out of him. He must have begun packing it the previous evening. It contained bathing trunks, t-shirts, shorts and underwear – all nice and neatly pressed. True, he was embarrassed but also as proud as a peacock. As if he thought that it was right for her to see that he was in the market again.

'Will it be the Canaries or Madeira this time? Did you intend to go away without saying a word to me? For how long have you been planning this?' she'd challenged him.

Obviously she received no answer. But Gertrude didn't need to know that. Not now at any rate.

Gertrud sighed at the other end of the telephone.

'He knows very well that he can always come to me if he wants a roof over his head,' she said.

'That's very kind of you. And yes, he does know it.'

But Håkan would never have taken up the standing invitation to spend the night in Gertrud's guest room in the event of a crisis. Or would he? At that moment Anna felt sure of nothing.

'Did he see you at the opera yesterday?' she asked.

'No. I don't think so. He only had eyes for that creature and was completely absorbed in her company. Perhaps I shouldn't say it but it struck me that he looked happy, almost euphoric, or however one can describe it.

Gertrud struggled to find the right words, but she didn't really need to. Anna already knew. When he came down into the kitchen after finishing his packing he'd looked different. As if his skin had been rejuvenated and tightened. And she knew that look on his face. The hunter was going hunting. His brown eyes didn't shine as clearly as before, but still ... The old rascal! Would he never give up?

Gertrud must have been thinking along the same lines.

'I don't understand how you put up with it.'

'Do I have a choice anymore?'

'You should never have allowed it to go on for so long,' Gertrud declared as if this was something that had never occurred to Anna.

But then she changed her tone and became like she was in the old days. She said she would come like a shot if Anna wanted her. She would just need to be met at the station. And she wanted to be kept informed about the situation. It wasn't good for Anna to be alone in her big house.

After the call finished she stayed sitting at her writing desk. As usual Gertrud had made her say more than she'd intended. But not absolutely everything. She kept a few details to herself. His passport had gone and he had taken his credit cards with him. It remained to be seen where he intended to travel and when the money would start to flow out. And whether Hilda Apeldoorn was high-maintenance or a respectable woman who paid her own way. And if he was now as free as a bird, why shouldn't she be?

There was to be another letter. But only a short one.

Dear Bo,

Quite unexpectedly, I have time to myself just now. Write me a line or let me know if you want to meet up? We could arrange somewhere halfway. What do you say to Sigtuna? I haven't been there for many years and it is obviously a little out of the way but I think there are good places to have lunch there for a reasonable price. What do you think about that?

Anna

Anna's letter lay unanswered in the middle draw of his writing desk. He would write to her as soon as he had been through the new material he had just received. It wouldn't do any harm to let her wait for a few days. But inwardly he could hear Marianne: 'Yes, yes! Hide behind your work as you always have done when you get into a tight corner. Escape into your old papers and maybe everything will sort itself out in the meantime. But remember, I am no longer with you and can't help you. You will have to sort this out yourself.' Obviously he would answer Anna's letter. Anything else would be cowardly and unforgiveable of him. But suddenly the thought didn't appeal. She knew too much about him. He had said too much in his letters. She also often said too much, though that was forgivable. He, of all people, had a lot of experience of how freely women talked. And there was something else – her suggestion that they should meet. On the whole he wanted to, but the small part of him that didn't want to was stubborn in its objection.

Sigtuna certainly sounded better than NK. But a tête-à-tête … He didn't know if he was ready for that. If he would ever be.

If he didn't get into something in the first place, he

wouldn't need to extricate himself. But Marianne had taught him that he wouldn't be able to look himself in the eye while shaving if he chose to live by evading difficult things. He had to say either yes or no to Anna's suggestion. But he could allow himself one day first to think about it.

Then he would have to make a decision one way or another. And after all, it wasn't a matter of life or death. They could meet and in the best case have a nice time together, and then let the whole thing peter out if they felt they had both had enough. Lunch at a restaurant didn't necessarily have to lead to new problems. He sat there with the writing paper in his hand and pondered.

Something in particular must lie behind her claim that she unexpectedly had time to herself. Had Håkan left for good or had she turned him out? And what did she expect from Bo, now?

The habitual caution that had annoyed Marianne so often came to the fore as he scrutinised the letter. He smiled a little at Anna's frugality. There was clearly no question of an expensive lunch out for them unless he insisted on issuing an invitation, which he would gladly have done. He had a feeling that she was living in adequate but straitened circumstances although he didn't know why. Perhaps because, as was well known, a translator's income was low; perhaps because, as he understood it, Håkan hadn't worked in a long time. His pension couldn't be very large.

There was a lot she didn't write about – good old Anna – even though her words flowed easily onto the page. What he liked about her – and would miss if it came to it – was her quiet feeling for the funny side of things. It was a sense of humour that Marianne wouldn't have appreciated; nor any of the girls except possibly Louise. That was why in spite of everything she was closest to his heart, the one who was a constant worry.

But she didn't have anything in common with Anna. He couldn't bracket them together in any other way. There were some people he didn't rightly know how to handle. Both Louise and Anna required some kind of support – obviously financial in Louise's case. In Anna's it was more difficult to define.

He was definitely not going to indulge in unnecessary speculation now. He would have time enough in her case. On the way home from the archive he would buy a plain postcard so that he could reply to her briefly.

He was able to drive out all thoughts of her while he was working – so much so that he forgot to buy the card. But he didn't forget to drop in to see Ellen. He thought it almost miraculous that an old person, who seen by all normal measures should have come to the end of her life, could recover and come home again. Obviously she was lucky to have met some skilled and clever doctors, and her will to live was enormous. She never gave up. But still he couldn't help being surprised.

Ellen was impatient when he arrived. She never could bear to wait for anyone. As a punishment she had planned some errands for him: a list of the books she wanted from the library in Fältöversten, and another of the things she needed from the ICA supermarket. Luckily he didn't have to go to the System store. Her elderly admirers made sure that there were bottles of alcohol in her home. He himself never had time to stop and drink a glass of sherry.

'Since you started running to the archive again, you have become so boring, almost as much as in Marianne's time,' she muttered, disappointed not to have his company.

He defended himself by saying that he had to meet up with his film club and was in a hurry. Then Ellen got it into her head that they would go together to an Irish film she was absolutely determined to see. Weren't there three performances at The Red Mill tomorrow?

It was when she became so eager for entertainment and, as it were, took it for granted that he would always be on hand, that he was frightened that her rehabilitation would be almost too successful. Suppose she became even more vigorous and in need of amusement than she already was? Where would it end?

It was then that he decided to have lunch with Anna. It would take up half a day including the travelling. Ellen must learn that he had a right to time on his own.

There were few people out that evening. Only the Berggrens and Kerstin had dared to come out and slip and slide around in the snow. That wasn't surprising since they were all getting on in years and generally cautious. There was a time when they used to discuss the film together afterwards over numerous glasses of red wine, but this evening they confined themselves to a quiet glass of beer at the nearest pub. They needed to fortify themselves for the journey home. The conversation was as always easy and Kerstin laughed her usual happy laugh, but Bo was thinking about Anna in her red house in that thinly populated area not so far from Stockholm. He had thought about her ever since he'd parted from Ellen; about her and Håkan. After some research he now knew a little more about her husband than Anna had told him. It might have been better to wait for her to give her version of how life turned out for them, he realised. More sporting, so to speak. And he wouldn't say that his curiosity had made him any the wiser, in spite of searching through civil and court records. He knew in which year Håkan had taken his law degree, in which courts he had worked and so on. At first it looked as though he had been on the way to a sparkling career but then it petered out. He became a provincial lawyer, changed firms a few times, and there didn't seem to be any more to it than that.

If there had been a scandal – which Bo doubted – then the Berggrens would have known something about it. Both of them were lawyers and must have been contemporaries of Håkan's at the high school, though there was no indication that they'd been classmates. Boys were called up for long periods at that time and their studies had to wait. He had thought of cautiously questioning them about Håkan, but so far nothing had come of it.

Then suddenly Bo heard himself saying, 'Do any of you remember a chap called Håkan Ljung who read law?'

There was silence for a moment, but not for long.

'I certainly do,' said Karin. 'We were in the same year more or less, me and him. And Olle of course, although Olle was on call-up for most of the time. Yes, I remember Håkan. Not easy to forget. Why are you asking?'

That was just the question that Bo had hoped to avoid. Now Kerstin was also interested and looking at him expectantly.

'I met his wife a few days ago, at a lunch, and she said that they had lived deep in the country for many years. But she didn't look much like a country woman to me. Neither did he as I remember him,' he lied. 'But that was a long time ago.'

'His wife?' said Kerstin. 'Did he marry that Gertrud or whatever she was called? No, that definitely finished. She got hold of a doctor instead if I remember correctly.'

'His wife is called Anna,' said Bo. 'I think she studied languages.'

Both Karin and Kerstin shook their heads. They couldn't remember an Anna.

'What did she look like,' asked Karin with curiosity. 'Pretty? He had a weakness for pretty girls.'

That wasn't an easy question to answer for someone who hadn't seen her close up.

'Tall,' he said. 'Quite thin. Perfectly presentable.'

'And nice, I hope,' said Kerstin. Since Marianne had died she had wanted to find someone for Bo, but hadn't so far been successful. Now her eyes were glinting.

'Are you interested?'

He shook his head.

'I can't imagine Håkan as some kind of country squire,' said Karin suddenly. 'He was such an intellectual. He wanted to debate things all the time. I can still see him with his pipe in his mouth and his eyebrows lifted sarcastically. Don't tell me that he has become old and fat?'

'He wasn't there.'

'Typical,' laughed Karin. 'He was never one to be on a lead. Nor someone whose hand you could hold when it thundered. But we were still a bit impressed by him. He had an answer for everything. We thought he would have a stellar career, didn't we Kerstin?'

'Indeed we did, but I didn't know him well. He wasn't my type.'

She smiled at Bo. They were good friends and she would gladly help him with any information as far as she could but she didn't have any. If her dear old Torbjörn had had the decency to die some years ago instead of slowly shaking apart with Parkinson's, it was not impossible that she would have stepped into Marianne's shoes.

'I wonder what became of him,' pondered Karin. 'He slipped away. But it was like that with most people. They moved and lost contact. They married and had children. There was no longer time to meet.'

There was a pink flush on her cheeks, the discussion seemed to have animated her. She smiled sympathetically at Bo and asked her husband, 'Do you know anything, Olle?'

'I remember a few things about the old devil,' he said. 'Strong jawed, a smooth operator, thought everything was his for the taking. Imagined he was something – but nothing came of it. A small-time city lawyer and then there was some scandal. I've forgotten what exactly. Money and women I assume. It's a long time since I heard anything about him. He disappeared early on. I thought he was dead.'

'No. He's not dead,' said Bo decisively.

Then the topic of conversation changed. But strangely the mood had altered. Nobody seemed to have anything much to say. Olle Berggren looked as though he was chewing over some old injury. His jaw was working and suddenly he rose to leave, taking Karin with him. 'Time to go home now,' he said, gripping her arm firmly. She rolled her eyes heavenwards at Bo and Kerstin. 'That's how it is, and there's nothing to be done about it,' she seemed to be saying.

Looking amused, Kerstin followed them with her eyes as they made their way to the exit.

'Can you explain why he behaved like that? Stiff in the legs and thin on top but clearly jealous as hell of something that happened long ago. We put our feet right in it there! There *was* something between Karin and Håkan once upon a time but I had completely forgotten about it. How on earth can Olle still feel put out after all this time? Karin has been an ideal wife to him – four children and a full-time job, and *still* she waits on him. Hardly even looks at anyone else. At least as far as I know. Men!' she said and shook her head. 'All of you like roosters!' she said. 'Will you never learn? And what plans do you have for this Anna? Better look out for Håkan if you have any. You saw what an effect just the sound of his name had on Olle.'

It had begun snowing harder while they had been sitting in the pub and the wind rose as he accompanied Kerstin home. Torbjörn peered out from behind the curtains of the living room but he didn't wave to them.

'Now he's annoyed,' sighed Kerstin. 'I have been out for too long. He will make himself heavy and impossible to handle when I help him into bed. You wouldn't believe how difficult he can be in order to punish me.'

'You don't have an easy time of it,' said Bo and gently stroked her cheek in the doorway where Torbjörn's eyes could no longer follow what he was doing.

'That's life. That's just how it is. But you must hurry up and find someone before it's too late. You are not suited to living on your own. I'm fond of you and I want you to be happy.'

Perhaps he should wait until Torbjörn disappeared from the scene and take Kerstin whom he had always been fond of and who wouldn't continually surprise and bewilder him with unpredictable statements. Simply give up on Anna.

Olle's tantrum had made him feel insecure. The Ljungs seemed more enigmatic than ever. While Bo walked on to take the underground railway home the wind was fierce, driving the snow around the houses. He had the feeling that snow like this could be a problem for a red farmhouse out in the sticks. He also thought about the two women he had just met. Neither Karin nor Kerstin – however well preserved they were or perhaps because of that – would ever have dreamed of shovelling snow and cutting wood. Anna on her own – if she still was – would be obliged to do both. How would she manage if the weather got worse?

After Marianne became ill and died he did not have the same confidence in women's ability to overcome difficulties as he had previously had. They might seem to be as strong as oxen but they were still the weaker sex.

Whether it had to do with the storm or because the evening had finished rather sadly he didn't know, but that night he slept badly and intermittently dreamed of Marianne, very clearly. It was the first time he had dreamed of her since her death. She was in a bad mood and looking for a little red jumper she had to finish knitting for one of the grandchildren. It was of vital importance that she found it and she made it clear to him that it was he who had mislaid it. He kept waking up and telling himself that he was only dreaming, Marianne was dead, but the dream kept coming back. It was all the more strange because Marianne had always kept her things in perfect order and was very even-tempered. Above all, it was disturbing that she should be so angry when he finally dreamed of her.

He was glad when it was morning and he could get up and dispel his troubled sleep with a shower. While he waited for the coffee to be ready he looked out of the window. Snow was lying thick on the road, cars half buried under it. Then he sat down to listen to the radio and the morning news summary of the catastrophes caused by the snowy weather. Svealand was the hardest hit. Half of Mälandalen was without electricity and Uppland was, as always, in a bad way. Lorries and buses were stuck and blocking some of the major roads. In other words, there was chaos in the snow just as there was every winter.

Obviously he should ring Anna and find out how she was, say thank you and yes to lunch, although it would be a day or two before they could get to Sigtuna. But it was too soon – he had no idea whether she was up bright and early in the mornings. It would be best to wait a bit anyway. He drank his coffee, toasted his bread and ate it with a lot of orange marmalade spread on it. At the same time he read the newspaper and lingered over it for as long as he could. He dressed, combed his hair in front of the mirror, made sure that there was no hair sprouting from his nose or ears, fixed what had to be fixed with tweezers and nail scissors and pulled a face under the operation.

He was as smart as he could be even if Anna wasn't able to see him. His heart was pounding and he pressed his hand against his chest until it calmed down. Then he fumbled as he dialled her number.

There were a few rings but then silence. He tried again, more carefully and precisely this time: there was no sound at all except for some weak clicking in the earpiece. On the third attempt the telephone seemed to be completely dead. It wasn't surprising considering the weather. But it was quite disturbing not to know how she was. He thought that it would be pure madness to get out on the road. Common sense told him that she would manage perfectly well by herself. She had managed well enough without him so far, so why shouldn't she be able to now? The neighbours would rally round if the bad weather continued. He could relax and get on with his Court of Appeal research. Anna would be all right.

Since she was a child Anna had been excited by bad weather. The threat to ordinary routine existence made her feel more alive. At last something was happening. She needed some drama in her life. For Håkan it was quite the opposite. He worried that tiles would be blown off, trees would fall, the whole roof would be lifted, the pipes would freeze and burst, or the shed door would come off its hinges and sail over the courtyard. He would never have been able to sleep on a night like the one she'd just passed. He would have lain awake imagining imminent catastrophe.

Now that Anna was alone in the old house it seemed that she had taken on some of the burden of anxiety. She woke up several times and listened to the storm. It whistled around the corners and shook the windows. The curtains moved gently in and out in the draught; it seemed as if they were breathing. It howled in the chimney and whirled through the tiled stove. Once she actually got up and looked out through the windows, first from her own room and then from Håkan's. The wind was north-easterly and by the light of the lamp on the gable end she could see the snow being swept from the roof of the storehouse and shed. At the front of the house it was packed high after being driven in from the fields. It would take

149

time to remove that drift. Every year Hilding had helped them to clear the snow away and had ploughed the road up to them. Now he had gone but Anton from Tuna could help instead. Things would work out one way or another.

She crept into bed again using Fabian as a hot water bottle. It was almost cosy lying under the duvet and listening to the storm. It was three o'clock. It wouldn't get any worse. The storm would abate towards morning if she remembered the weather forecast correctly. She was completely safe. No one could take her from the house. It was just her and the snow and the storm.

The next time she woke up everything was quiet. Melted snow had frozen on the lowest panes of the window and the reluctant dawn was spreading a grey daylight through the room. It was cold outside the bedclothes. The power had gone but the radio worked on batteries. The morning news was almost entirely about the bad weather in the night. Trees had fallen across lines, trains were standing still and cars lying in ditches. She listened with interest and a certain fascination, still exhilarated by the weather's onslaught.

The house hadn't yet gone cold and lukewarm water was coming from the hot tap on the washbasin. Then it gave out. She quickly washed herself in the small amount of water she'd salvaged and put on some warm clothes. It was already ice-cold on the stairs. It was always cold there in the winter. The gaps between the steps let in cold air from the crawl space beneath.[26] It should have been better insulated but nothing had been done – nothing was ever done.

It was warmer in the kitchen. She hurried over to get the wood burning stove going. It was always kept loaded with kindling for emergencies. Thin grey smoke rose from the stove rings before the wood began to crackle seriously. It wasn't long before there was a roaring in the stove pipe. While she waited for the coffee water to boil, she forced Fabian out. The snow resisted and she had to push the kitchen door open with her shoulder. He reluctantly climbed through the gap in the door and lifted his short legs as high as possible as he climbed through the snow to the dry clematis on the gable.

The wind had begun to blow again and was now coming directly from the north. The temperature had gone down to minus five and small pointed snowflakes were landing on Fabian's coat. They melted as soon as he came into the kitchen again. It was beautifully white outside. Everything was submerged, rounded and soft. The birds were silent and invisible.

She went around the lower rooms and checked on the situation through the windows. All the trees were still standing but a large branch had fallen from the sycamore tree and was lying across the entrance to the earth cellar. One of the black doors of the storehouse had been blown off and was hanging askew from its hinge, but there had been no real damage. The snow was just a sprinkling on the leafless birch twigs. She looked across the fields deeper into open country. Not a single light came from the farms at the edge of the forest. None of them had power. No telephone either. Hers was dead. She couldn't even hear a crackle when she lifted up the receiver. In its way it was a relief. She was free from the eternal wait for the call that never came. Even if he wanted to, Håkan couldn't reach her. She could dismiss him from her mind with a clear conscience. It felt like a well-deserved break from everyday life.

She drank her morning coffee with a strange feeling of satisfaction. This was the life... or rather, this was also the life. There was nothing to struggle with. Nothing real or tangible to avoid. She would manage and in her thoughts she was already describing her lonely struggle with the elements in a letter to Bo, while she ate an extra sandwich to give her strength for the day's work ahead. Then she wondered if there was anyone in the whole world who was thinking about her. It was unlikely that Håkan would wherever he was. Perhaps Lasse out in Värmland. He at least knew what the snow could do, but he didn't know that Håkan had run away and he would think that his mother could manage as always. 'Mum with speed lines' he called her when he was a schoolboy. Bo must have received her suggestion about lunch by now. He could forget that at the moment. There would be no lunch out for anyone until the roads were cleared. He probably couldn't imagine how difficult it could be living out in the sticks.

Malin in Brussels had certainly forgotten what snow was. That is to say real Swedish snow in huge drifts, not tourist snow in the Alps. And Agneta, her sister, was probably as much without power and snowed in as she was, but she had her sweet old Hugo with her, plus tractors and people. She didn't know that Håkan was away and Hilding dead.

Gertrud in Stockholm didn't have enough imagination to think of anyone being snowed in and without power on a lonely farm. She would just look out of her window, shudder and decide to stay in until the roads were cleared and sanded. Just like all Anna's old friends in the city.

In some vague way she felt superior to them, both physically and morally. Say what you will about her, she wasn't afraid of hard work. But she was feeling more determined than exhilarated when she went out with double-thickness socks in her boots, wearing a thick winter jacket and a woollen hood on her head. The large snow shovels were obviously in the garage. She just had to plod over there. She stood still for a moment and looked around. It was actually worse than she had expected. The drive up to the garage was a single hard packed snow drift and the hedge around the garden had changed into a thick white wall. On the other side the field, ditch and road had been blown together into a white desert. She was literally cut off from the rest of the world. No post, no newspaper, no telephone.

First of all she must manage to get to the woodshed. Without wood there was no heat and who knew when the power would come on again. She took up the shovel and then discovered that the snow was much heavier than she had expected. This was snow that had melted and frozen again. It took a long time to clear a path from the kitchen door to the shed.

An hour later she had cut a large supply of wood and was depressed to realise that she wasn't as quick and efficient as she had imagined. She was a tired old grandmother, without speed lines, as she dragged the old-fashioned wood basket to the kitchen door and then piled the neatly chopped wood under the stove. She made several more trips to the wood shed, and then it was time for coffee and an hour's rest.

The wood stove was giving out a delightful warmth in the kitchen, but in the hall the temperature had sunk to 10C. In the living room she had to light the open fire to prevent the flowers – such as they were – from freezing to death. It was also good to get a fire going in the study as well, even if she didn't manage to write a line.

She fried an egg and ate a sandwich. Then she drank mug after mug of coffee. It enabled her to summon her strength and then use it sparingly. The most important thing was to have a large store of wood in the house. She would look for the kick-sledge so that she could transport the wood basket without needing to struggle with it.

The kitchen radio had no batteries and she made her weary way up to take the radio from her bedroom so that she could hear the latest news about the weather. But it seemed that no one was interested in the snow and the power cuts any longer. There was foreign news of all kinds, refugee crises in Africa, war and misery. She muttered quietly to herself. They should sit in their radio station without power, freezing cold, and then they would find out what fun it was. Then perhaps they could do a little more than just reporting that at least four thousand homes in Mälardalen were still without power.

If Håkan had been at home there would have been two people to deal with the snow and chop the wood. He must have had a premonition of what was coming because he'd timed his departure so cleverly. Slowly she worked herself up into a mighty rage against him, the eternal deserter.

While her fury mounted she went out to the woodshed again and cut a new supply of wood. She took the largest blocks and vented her anger on them. It is remarkable what an old woman could do when anger is sticking in her craw. Carrying a basket in each hand, she stumbled over Fabian on the way to the kitchen entrance. He retreated with his tail between his legs when she tumbled over onto the snow. His tail didn't come up again until she had stopped swearing. Even then he wasn't sure that she wasn't dangerous and trembled a little. But that could come from the cold, she told herself. He couldn't busy himself as usual while the snow was lying like a cold odourless cover over all his store of interesting smells.

They went back together into the kitchen and he lay down under the table and gnawed on an old bone while she drank tea. She thought about what might have happened if she had injured herself in the fall or slipped with the axe and cut her leg. She was living dangerously. All people on their own lived dangerously. Life itself was dangerous.

She sat at the kitchen table and looked out again and again at the oak-tree hill as if by an act of will she could summon Hilding's tractor. But she didn't hear so much as a whisper. It wasn't likely that anyone was thinking of her. It wasn't clear that anyone around here knew that Håkan was away. She wasn't obviously a deserving case. 'You're still going strong then,' Hilding used to say when he found her up on a ladder painting the house or cutting the grass in front of the shed with a scythe. She was a superwoman who managed in all weathers. That was the picture of herself she had created. Now she had only herself to blame.

Suddenly the light over the table came on. It flickered for a moment and then went dark again. But it showed that somebody somewhere was trying to get the power back again.

Her strength returned and she got up from the table. She felt stiff and sore in all her limbs as she put on her outdoor clothes once more. She would clear a path down to the post-box at the roadside to avoid having to plod out in her nightclothes and dressing gown to get the newspaper if the road had now been ploughed and the post could get through. She could already envisage the morning with freshly brewed coffee and a newspaper for company.

At about four o'clock, just as it was beginning to get dark, the power came back. The boiler in the utility room clicked on and the light above the freezer shone green and bright. She stood there feeling happy and looking at all the small lights which showed life was going back to normal. The fridge was working. The shipping forecast was coming out of the radio – strong winds and poor visibility. The digital clock above the oven started to tick. Water came out of the taps. The pipes wheezed and coughed a bit and then all was back to normal. She could feel the warmth slowly creeping back into the radiators. She switched on the electric kettle and the indicator light glowed orange, which meant it was working. She warmed up some milk on the stove just to enjoy seeing the plate glowing red. The electric supply was well under way – up to and including the little light on the bell of the outer door. It glowed self-importantly as if someone might come past and press the button.

She went round and turned on both inside and outside lights and at the same time she noticed that the lights were on at the farms at the edge of the forest. It gave her a feeling of security. Even she had forgotten how vulnerable the infrastructure was, how quickly a house can become cold and how literally heavy life became if the technology failed.

She sat down at the kitchen table with her mug of instant coffee. It was already dusk and the roads had not been ploughed.

The highways authority wasn't doing anything. And Hilding was dead.

But sooner or later someone would realise that she was snowed in. The postwoman ought to sound the alarm. She had saved elderly men and women before when their cottages were snowed in, and hadn't been fazed by it.

As expected the telephone was silent. She managed not to imagine it ringing when she filled up the bath tub. A really hot bath was what she needed after the day's hard work. She had sometimes been freezing and sometimes sweating and if a rescue team should presume to come out, she wanted to meet them clean in body and soul.

'A really tough old lady,' she thought as she saw her reflection in the bathroom mirror. Her cheeks were glowing after an hour's work with the axe and shovel. As healthy as a *vinterny*[27] – whatever that was. But when she looked more closely she thought that she looked more like an old winter apple, red certainly but also wrinkled and with brown flecks on her skin. Her hair hung down in long rat's-tails, lank with dried sweat. The rest was collarbone, bones, tendons and dried out wrinkly skin. It was as if everything soft and rounded on her slid lower and lower with the passing years.

The frame of the mirror mercifully cut off her reflection just before her breasts. 'A devastated landscape,' she thought as she climbed clumsily into the bathtub. The water was so hot that she could only lower herself in a little at a time until finally she was covered by the surprisingly cool lather with its sweet scent. That was thanks to Malin who regularly supplied her parents with an assortment of luxury bars of soap, bath foam, cream and perfumes from all the tax-free shops she encountered on her trips.

Anna washed her hair, rinsed it under the shower and wound a hand-towel round her head. She leaned back in the bath and shut her eyes. Once or twice she almost fell asleep but couldn't persuade herself to get out. She lay back in the bathtub without a single thought in her head. She let in more hot water from time to time, infinitely grateful that the power was on again.

Eventually she had to get out. It wasn't so easy. But by

pulling hard on the side of the bath she managed. Then she felt a sharp pain in her back. It was as sharp as a knife then it subsided. She was able to lift her legs over the side of the bath and climb out. Bathrooms, and particularly bathtubs, were deadly for the elderly, she thought. With bad luck you could end up lying on the floor. All it took was a momentary slip.

But she had managed.

At first she felt warm after the bath, but a little later she felt frozen and began to have further pain in her back. She should obviously have had a cold shower but didn't want to now. Time for lunch for her and Fabian. She soaked some dried dog food for him and then whisked up some soup for herself. A meat extract cube, tomato purée, and a little cream – generously laced with sherry. There was so little left in the bottle that it wouldn't have been enough to offer anyone. That is if someone did come with the snow plough. Anyway, countrymen preferred cognac or brandy. Sherry was too feminine a taste for them. But with her it went down a treat. She felt warm again and hopeful.

She was in full control of the situation. She wasn't so badly snowed in that she couldn't put on her skis and go over to other people if she really wanted to. And she was clean and smelled good, almost pleasantly tired after the shovelling. If it hadn't been for the grinding ache in her back …. But it went away when she sat in front of the fire and watched *Rapport* with Fabian next to her. She nodded at pictures of roads snowed up again, at vehicles in ditches and men with power saws standing around fallen fir trees, at thick wet snow on branches. She thought that she had never seen such an interesting news report before. This was what it meant for humanity to be exposed to winter. Here she sat, an elderly woman on her own, completely cut off from other people. But was she afraid? Not a bit!

She went to bed early but had difficulty in sleeping. The old house creaked and groaned and she ended up listening to the sounds. Mice ran around in the roof space. Their tiny claws clattered above her. The bare branches of the Virginia creeper near the window scratched at the panes like a child's hand when the wind got up. Someone was shut out. Someone wanted to come in. *Wuthering Heights* – Heathcliff and Cathy. She wasn't lying comfortably. Her right shoulder was hurting from the snow-shovelling. Fabian was also restless. He kept on jumping off the bed and then on again. Each time he pushed up to her and she changed sides with difficulty. Her hips were hurting. Her back was stiff. Fabian felt heavy and big-footed when he climbed over her and trampled round and round until he could find a comfortable sleeping position. Then he became restless again, sat up and stared hard at the window. He growled a little, deep in his throat and heard something that she couldn't. Perhaps it was a fox, perhaps a dog a long way away.

Towards morning she dropped off and slept deeply and dreamlessly with Fabian up close to her back. She woke to the sound of an engine. The sky was grey and it was almost eight o'clock. There must be a tractor on the road! She sat up in bed and stretched out for her dressing-gown on the chair near her bed.

Then she felt pain in her back. And this time it was serious. She stood bent forward like a clasp knife and couldn't move up or down. The pain was so severe that she had black spots in front of her eyes and thunder in her ears. She held firmly onto the back of a chair until she could see again. Then she slowly slid down onto her knees with her arms around the chair and then cautiously moved herself to the floor where she stayed lying on her stomach. There was still thundering and buzzing in her ears and stars flickered in front of her eyes. She had never previously been struck with back pain of this severity. It was almost unbearable.

But it wasn't dangerous. It would go away provided she didn't move and was patient about lying completely still.

So gradually the thundering in her ears went away and she could make out the window again. She listened but couldn't hear anything outside. If someone had been coming with a snow plough to clear away the snow he couldn't possibly have finished already and gone away. There would be rumbling, scraping and booming. It must have been a wishful dream that woke her up. Or possibly an aeroplane or perhaps more likely a helicopter looking for fallen power lines.

She moaned quietly with her face pressed against the bedside mat. When she opened her eyes she saw the room from an unusual perspective. Fluff balls under the bed, and stuck between the bed and the wall with half its cover visible was *Århundradets Ordmusik.* And she hadn't even missed it! When had she last used the vacuum cleaner?

She shut her eyes again and whimpered forlornly to herself. Then Fabian began to dance around her on his short legs. He barked a bit and licked her cold sweaty neck in encouragement. She couldn't fend him off because she dared not move. And he couldn't understand why she was lying there. She had never done that before. But she kept lying there and lying there and after a while he lay down next to her and slept.

A few hours later she succeeded in shuffling herself out of the room on her hands and knees and went down the stairs on her stomach feet first then crept towards the outside door. Then she slowly heaved herself up with the help of a chair and the windowsill until she could turn the latch and press down the handle. Fabian was at her feet, almost desperate by now, with his shoulder against the door. Together they got it open.

In this situation she realised that it wasn't she who was the problem. It was him. He didn't show any consideration when he had to go out. And he had right on his side. She had taught him to let her know. And he had done that. After he woke up, he continuously ran up and down the stairs, threw himself against the outer door, and whined persistently. She understood how he felt. It was the same for her. She shuffled into the toilet at the back of the cloakroom. The whole procedure was so painful that she felt nauseated, but when she came out again wearing a thick dressing gown and having washed her face, she felt a little better. She had tied her hair up in a ponytail. She now looked respectable. It would have been dreadful to have been found by Anton from Tuna lying on the floor in her crumpled nightclothes, sweaty and unappealing. It wasn't impossible that by and by he would come out on his tractor when someone reminded him that neither she nor Håkan were to be seen. 'The old woman was lying there showing everything she'd got,' he might well have thought of saying when he later described the scene that awaited him.

With great difficulty and very slowly, she succeeded in putting on the kettle and shaking out some dog food. There was water in the dog bowl. That was lucky as she could avoid bending down. Fabian was busy using up his pent-up energies in the garden. She could see him attacking twigs that had been blown down, taking them by surprise and killing them. He rushed around in the snow then came to a dead stop and stared at the door. Why wasn't she coming out? Wasn't there going to be a walk?

She shuffled to the door and called him in but she didn't lock up after him. If rescue was on the way, they shouldn't have to break in if she wasn't able to open the door. Then she made herself a cup of hot instant coffee. She didn't have the strength to get herself any bread and anyway she wasn't hungry. She left the lamp on over the kitchen table so that it looked as though the house was lived in. Then she struggled up the stairs on her stomach again and went into the bathroom. There were pain-killing tablets there and something a little stronger – distalgesic. She swallowed two tablets and crawled back to her room. She pushed the bottle of distalgesic tablets and her toothbrush mug filled with water along the floor in front of her. Once she had reached the bed she was faced with a real ordeal – she had to get up onto it.

Sweating and exhausted, she stayed lying on the floor and waited motionlessly for the pain to recede. She saw the strangest patterns behind her eyelids: exploding suns, rockets and orange slices that spurted blood. But then the fireworks calmed down. So long as she didn't move she was almost free from pain. If she could stop worrying about Fabian's rightful demands she was almost all right. But he would make demands and she would have to open the door at least twice more.

The next time she woke up it was almost dark outside. She was lying in the same position as she did when she slept: on her right side with her leg slightly angled. She was fixed in that position and so long as she didn't move she felt no pain. The most important thing was to keep still, to lie there as though she were dead and let time pass.

Then the anger came welling up. What did Håkan mean

by leaving her like this? What did he mean by staying away? He had no sense of responsibility and had never had any. He might at least have come home to look after Fabian. He really liked the dog. And would it have been so impossible to bring her a cup of tea, tea with sugar and lemon, even if he had never done so before? But had he ever been there when she needed him? No. And no again. She had always had to do everything herself. She had been alone in all of life's crises. Where had he been when the children were born? He followed her to the maternity hospital and then went to the cinema. He wouldn't have been of any use and women giving birth were not particularly aesthetically pleasing. Those were different times and childbirth was not for fathers then. But still ...

She knew that she was being unfair. That they had shared at least some of the worries and troubles. But that didn't really help. Mostly she had been left alone to solve the problems. It could be that she'd kept him out of things because it was simpler that way. He didn't get involved even once. He could put up with very little that was taxing; had to protect himself. And then there were all those women. That Dutch one had clearly succeeded in breathing life into him again after the recent years of inertia. Anna had thought that he'd accepted a slower pace of life. But he hadn't. He still had to show that he was up to it.

All that deceit... But nothing to compare with what he had exposed her to by creeping away into illness and avoiding further responsibility, an illness so vaguely defined that it barely had a name but that freed him from everything that was troublesome or tedious.

So she managed. She had learned how to. He had been cared for and looked after, never gave anything back, just took it for granted that everything was as it should be.

Rage boiled inside her. Not for a very long time had she let out her anger. She was raging as she had when she was a small child. It would really serve him right if he came home and found her here dead in her bed. Then he would have to look after himself and see how much fun it was! She didn't believe he would get a new woman who was sane, however much he wanted that. His euphoric state would last perhaps three or four weeks before he crash-landed. And then he would be alone again. She could see him standing over her, taken aback by the sight of her dead body: Håkan the eternal innocent. And if he was asked how he could not have known that she was ill? No one had told him so it wasn't his fault, he would say. Just as nothing else that went wrong over the years had been his fault. He was ill.

She had noticed early on that he was unbalanced, but refused to accept that it was anything serious. He was after all very clever, a naturally intelligent person. She confronted him, told him to sharpen up and pull himself together – as idiotic as quarrelling with someone who had cancer or diabetes. No, it wasn't his fault that he brought disgrace on himself and his profession and that it also affected her by association. It wasn't his fault that the children were exposed to both contempt and offensive sympathy and that friends withdrew. But in the middle of that chaos Gertrud sailed in, rolled up her sleeves and cleaned the house, gave the youngsters dinner when they came home from school and stood by them like a rock amidst the confusion of the worst times. One could never forget that, even when she was at her most intolerable subsequently, Anna said to herself, lying there and letting the difficult memories wash over her.

No, nothing was ever Håkan's fault but it was still difficult to forgive him. Many more troubles followed in the wake of his first breakdown. But mental illness is no more morally contemptible than influenza, Anna reminded herself.

He had just had the wrong parents and couldn't possibly be blamed for that. How could he have known that there was mental instability in his lineage. And that this was what made life on the mission station so inexplicably difficult. It seemed his mother interpreted it as God's punishment. How could it be his fault that his childhood had been so difficult that he had to tell lies about it? His parents' death was the best thing that could have happened to him, he once said.

But it wasn't that simple.

Now that he was largely cured and had been healthy for many years, Anna couldn't really reproach him for having been ill. Even less for the fact that the cure itself had changed him. The quickness and intensity that had once been his most attractive traits had disappeared. There were no longer any highs or lows except for those increasingly rare and short-lived periods when he woke up and wanted to live life as far away as possible from his wife and home.

How he perceived himself deep down, she didn't know. But she didn't think that he was tortured by shame over his capsized legal career. Those who are not completely healthy cannot work. It's difficult enough just to live.

She didn't think that he remembered his most spectacular misdeeds while suffering from psychosis. Perhaps it was just as well. But others still remembered them and *schadenfreude* was never far away. They hadn't many friends left.

It was good that they had the farmhouse. They could live there all year round and avoid being seen in the street or meeting people they knew. Or see acquaintances crossing the street to avoid meeting them. It was just as well they had their retreat when reality became a burden.

And the children – it was difficult to know how deeply his illness had affected them. There was no question of keeping it quiet or pretending everything was normal. Anna gave honest answers to their questions. But they didn't often ask and did not give too much trouble. That would certainly have been too much to bear – mental illness and teenage rebellion. Anyway she liked to think that the difficult years drew them together in some way. Malin and Lasse had a particularly good relationship with each other.

Strangely enough, she had never worried about Håkan's condition being inherited by the children. When they were born he was stable if self-centred, touchy and quick to lose his temper. Similar to her, if she was honest. With the difference that mothers do not have time to be particularly self-absorbed, if they are going to get anything done. She never worried about their inheriting it. Lasse was like her own father, confident and stable, clever but not particularly quick-witted. Malin was certainly selfish but not gloomy – quite the opposite.

And the little one who died had been gone so long it was as if she had never been. That thought in itself was so upsetting that tears ran down Anna's cheeks. There was no end to her sensitivity when she opened the floodgates.

How many – if any – were left of the amorous fiancées and newlyweds Håkan had seen as his great mission in life to seduce? She'd once believed that her love would make up for everything he'd suffered: traumatic childhood, being an outsider and then the loneliness of his boarding school years.

She wondered what was left of her goodwill now. Not

much probably, but it had endured a long time, perhaps because she was so naïve and stubborn. He would have been all right without her and both of them would probably have been successful. In the long run, a comfortable home life was too tame for him. Certainly he'd got on well with her – she was a pleasant and stable girl – but no man was ever particularly proud to be seen out with her. Women like that were easily to be found elsewhere. He had found them in order to put some excitement into his life. But she had told herself they weren't significant because he was also home-loving and very fond of the children.

It didn't bother her for very long that she had been deserted. He was still her children's father if not her soul-mate. After that neither of them tried to make the other happy. She thought that it would have gone better if she had occasionally stroked his cheek; put an arm around his shoulders when times were difficult. Shown him a little tenderness.

Probably she didn't give him enough of anything. The well of affection had dried up permanently. There were angry years, bitter years, before she had learned to accept the situation. And she couldn't blame her faults and deficiencies and bad temper on her childhood as he did. Because she had had a good childhood. No one could say anything to the contrary. It had been secure.

She was so miserable as she lay there in bed that she cried over that as well, she who in spite of herself was dried up and without feelings. Because her childhood had certainly been happy, but perhaps not as happy as her sisters. Agneta and Harriet were older, always first to try everything new and exciting. And such sweet girls, so much sweeter than she had been. Anna trotted behind in their footsteps, angry and

sulking because no one really bothered about her. She was
certainly loved, but obviously not as much as her sisters. She
didn't come into the same category as them. She was the child
who brought up the rear, for whom the parents didn't really
have the strength or the sisters the time. They would have
been satisfied with each other.

It was perhaps not so surprising that she was angry. She
remembered mostly feeling anger, not spitefulness. She must
have suppressed it. Jolly and pleasant outside, naughty at home,
it was called. There must have been some explanation for
why she preferred to play in other people's yards and in other
people's playrooms. Perhaps it was just boring at home.

Later it turned out that she could not handle boys as easily
and elegantly as her sisters. She might have been expected
to learn from them. They fell head over heels in love with
unbridled enthusiasm and from the beginning were quite clear
that they belonged to the chosen ones, the ones to aspire to. It
was the opposite with her. She was convinced that she would
be scorned and rejected but she still had certain expectations.
There was no question of her being satisfied with someone
that no one else wanted. It was all rather awkward and sad.
Agneta and Harriet got married appropriately and respectably.
There were no in-laws who could not be mentioned. All her
sisters' children were also successful and in their turn married
wisely and well. The families stayed together although Harriet
had been dead for ten years. Now they met at Agneta's house.
Sweet, kind, good-natured Agneta who by this point was on
the verge of being canonized by relatives and friends. Harriet
was certainly sweeter but not as kind and therefore more fun.
Anna still missed her. Harriet had also been fond of Malin and
not in the least shocked by her free living.

Anna thought of all her nieces and nephews, all married, all with their own children, all securely settled within a reasonable distance of their parents, kind and responsible.

Then she shed a tear of pure jealously and felt a ridiculous twinge of bitterness that even in this moment of clarity she did not have any amorous escapades to regret, that she'd never cut loose and gone on a spree. She had had the inclination and the desire but never, ever, the opportunity. A woman who sits at home at her writing desk and has a limited circle of friends, rarely meets anyone to fall in love with. There was no moral superiority behind her faithfulness, only a shortage of possible objects. She had never found love easy.

Two days later the roads had been cleared and apart from the piled-up drifts of dirty snow, it was as if there had never been a storm. When the morning rush hour was over Bo was sitting in his car on his way out of town. There was more slush than he had expected on the E18, but it was not particularly worrying. He just had to be on his guard. Like most car owners, he thought that he drove well. Confident, focussed and with a feeling for the state of the road and the traffic. He had never committed any traffic offences, obviously with the exception of parking tickets. He had never driven over anyone, never crashed into anyone, never ran off the road, never been stopped for speeding and never driven after drinking. He had once been hit heavily from behind but in that case was completely innocent.

Perhaps he didn't now drive as fast as he used to, but he believed that he kept up a steady speed and no one needed to swear at him. Still there had been a couple of occasions recently when he had been overtaken by some racers who stuck up their fists in what he believed was called an obscene gesture, suggesting that slow-coaches like him had no business to be on the road. That disturbed him a lot. He continued to believe that he drove excellently and avoided all risk-taking.

He gave up pursuing cars that overtook him just to show that he could do the same as them. No, there was no real reason why he should stop driving. Old age was no obstacle. There was nothing wrong with his reaction times, and if contrary to all expectations there should be, he could compensate for that with experience.

But the roads were not as clear as he had expected. There was a lot of snow remaining on the verges and the surface was rutted and slushy. Every time he was overtaken he received a shower of opaque slush on his windscreen and was driving blind until the windscreen-wipers had cleared it away. Before Bålsta there were roadworks and speed restrictions and no overtaking for several kilometres. After having been chased by lorries, buses and speeding vehicles in general, he found it restful to have 70 k.p.h. as a cruising speed.

When he later turned onto a minor road, the situation immediately became serious. It hadn't been salted or sanded and was still completely covered with snow. It was a long time since he had driven on such a surface. That was real winter driving and his studded tyres were not much to shout about. He pondered a little about how he could explain to his daughters how he came to be there if an accident happened. There was nothing wrong with his car, nor with his driving, but the tyres did not seem to keep a grip on the road. A skid was waiting to ambush him. In his mind he could hear Ulrika cross-examining him as he sat in a wheelchair at the hospital. 'Dear Papa, what were you doing there?'

She was the one who was most like Marianne. Clever, brave and persistent. But sometimes he thought that she had also inherited Marianne's negative attributes to an unfortunate extent. But that's how it was. It was the snub nose, the big ears and the crooked teeth that she had inherited. Not the warm expression, the curly hair and the dimples in the cheeks. It was the same way with her character traits. Or is it always the case that one takes the good ones for granted and notices only the bad? In this case, it was Ulrika's way of locking onto a question with bulldog-like stubbornness when she wanted an answer that he was thinking of.

After a few miles on the winter road it felt as though he had gone back in time. Conditions were just like this one year when they spent Christmas with Marianne's parents in the large villa outside Hedemora. The three youngsters had been on the backseat of the car and Marianne next to him. The roads were narrow and winding. At every fifth mile there had been an accident. The victims lay lined up at the roadside, the car or cars were crumpled in the ditch, and a scattered crowd of helpful people were putting blankets on the victims. The sight was enough to drive away all yuletide merriment.

Marianne obviously tried to stop the children from seeing anything and understanding what was going on. She was a master at seeing elves and trolls, moose and eagles behind spruces and trees. The children followed her pointing finger with screwed up eyes but still didn't miss the drama at the roadside. He could almost hear their voices: 'Papa, why are they lying there?' 'Papa, what happened to those cars?' 'Papa, was it blood, that red stuff on the snow?' And Louise, the smallest, with her nose pressed up against the side window, 'Papa, were they all dead?'

Driving used to be more dangerous, winter accidents numerous. At least two on the road to the Christmas celebration and a similar number, or more, coming back. Still they always set out full of confidence, without seat-belts or children's car seats, and with the vehicle packed full of Christmas presents, cellulose wadding – Louise took her time becoming dry – suitcases, toys, books, an incredible number of boots, ski boots, outdoor clothing, hats, gloves and scarves. Marianne sang, told stories, invented riddles, scolded when necessary and handed out biscuits for general sedation until the car was full of crumbs. She had been tireless. And when he sat behind the wheel, he was Papa who couldn't be disturbed because then anything could happen. Responsibility for the family's safety rested on him. His word was law. He liked that. Even the ambulances appearing with their howling sirens and bright lights – there were no blue lights as far as he could remember – were stimulating. Memento mori. They strengthened the feeling of being alive.

He also thought about the Christmas celebrations. The whole big family that got together every year with children and grandchildren and all the small cousins lying packed high on mattresses in every slanted corner of the attic. His daughters all had happy memories of Christmas, different though they were from his own. He enjoyed Christmas almost more than the children, despite the constant sibling rivalry in the different generations. A community for good and ill, said Marianne. She noticed almost only the good, didn't want to notice anything else.

That was how it was so long as his parents-in-law were alive. Then it finished. There were too many heirs, too many with strong wills. The villa was sold and that was the end of it.

He was thinking about all that while he was driving and felt a little melancholy. He and Marianne had not created anything like that for their grandchildren. What they would remember of their mother's parents would probably be the

173

weeks when their grandmother lay dying. That natural death among all her loved ones, which he'd had such a hard time accepting. But Marianne wanted it that way.

The driving had become easier. He was no longer worried about the road conditions. He had a seatbelt, front-wheel drive and also fifty years' driving experience behind him. He thought the whole thing was exciting.

There had been other occasions when he had driven on that road, but now he was not coming from curiosity but out of a feeling of responsibility. Anna had sent a kind of call for help. That was the way her letter must surely be read.

But it had taken a while before he'd realised that and her telephone line was still down. It was not impossible that he would drive the long journey there unnecessarily. There was nothing to indicate that she was sitting waiting for him in her red house. She could be at the dentist, visiting her bosom friend, the formidable Gertrud, or taking the dog for a walk.

But he didn't really believe that. He had realised that she was genuinely in need in one way or another. That was why he was defying snow and slush. He couldn't be responsible for leaving her silence uninvestigated. Marianne would never have forgiven him for that. 'A sense of responsibility is what separates us from animals,' she insisted. But how could she have known that?

The most important question of course was what Anna would say when she saw him. If she were at home.

He had a bunch of tulips well wrapped up on the seat next to him. They were fresh and 'crisp' – a new word in his vocabulary. Women can always be given flowers. It is rarely taken badly.

He didn't think about what he would say. That would look

after itself when the moment came. It wasn't a good idea to plan too far in advance and keep repeating things by rote. Anything could go wrong then.

It troubled him a little that Håkan might be standing on the doorstep to receive him. In that case Bo would ask for someone fictitious and leave as quickly as possible. But probably it would be Anna who made contact with the outside world. What would be would be.

For a moment he was slightly worried that he had lost his way. The landscape didn't look the same as the last time he was there. Then there had been sunshine, frost and bare ground. The autumn wheat had still been gleaming green in the fields. Now it was overcast and everything was covered in snow. The fir trees along the road were weighed down. The farmhouses and the barns were a dull pale red, almost brownish and over them lay the roofs heavy and white with snow. But he had come the right way. The little church lay in front of him pointing a warning to the sky with its tapering tower. No paths to the churchyard were visible, all surfaces softly rounded by the snow. The gravestones were sparse, white on the windward side. A tractor on the car park was pushing the snow away. A high bank of it had been piled up against the churchyard wall.

He followed the same narrow path past the church and down to the sea as he had taken on the previous occasion. Exactly as he remembered, it ran down to a little area of cottages and ended at a turning circle with a long row of post-boxes that all had snow caps on top. By all accounts only summer people lived there.

Beyond the turning circle the road wasn't ploughed. Where it was sheltered by the spruces, you could clearly see its course before it disappeared between the open fields. Everything was covered with packed-down snow. There was no possibility of going any further.

So that was the situation.

He turned round and drove back. The sky had become even more grey and heavy with snow. All his hopes and determination had evaporated. It was only a sense of obligation that made him stand next to the tractor on the car park and get out of the car. A young man with a three-day stubble opened the door and leaned towards him. He had an open face and a very friendly voice. Bo thought that he would make an ideal kindergarten teacher for small fatherless boys to identify with. But perhaps he was most useful on the tractor.

Initially they talked a bit about the weather. That came naturally. It was always the first topic of conversation. Then Bo talked about where he was going and said that he hadn't got there.

'Fasicken is the same,' said the man in his friendly voice. 'The Swedish Road Authority doesn't look after that bit. Hilding used to look after them. But he isn't there anymore. He died.'

He paused briefly out of respect and Bo could also see in the untouched snow tracks of big boots on the way to eternity.

'Yes. They are stuck there where they are, but they are not in any danger. They have light and warmth. None of us has the telephone on again yet, but if there was something wrong Anna would put on her skis and come over to us. She isn't the sort of person to make a fuss about a bit of snow.'

'Have you actually seen anyone moving around in the house?' asked Bo.

'We don't need to stand and stare at each other through binoculars. There are lights on in the house and that is enough for me.'

'When will the road become passable, do you think?' Bo enquired cautiously.

He understood very well that he was speaking with a free Swedish farmer who would not under any circumstances take orders from a nobody – and that was how Bo was perceived. He could feel it in the air. But he had to know if Anna would have to sit in that house like a prisoner until the thaw came with the spring.

'They'll be sorted out. If we can find the time. There are people who are in a worse position than Anna and Håkan. But they are not exactly young and we will look after them. It is difficult for old people in these circumstances.'

He was emphasising their old age unnecessarily. As if he enjoyed dwelling on the difference between them and himself – a strong young man on a tractor – and a moss-covered pair like Anna and Håkan. Bo knew that this disparagement was directed at him as well, an interfering old Stockholmer.

'If you see them could you please convey my greetings? Bo Rydeman,' he said firmly.

But he didn't in the least believe that his greeting would be passed on to Anna. The man's disarming friendly voice probably had little to do with a genuinely kind heart. It was more likely just his dialect. Bo decided he would ask Anna when he had the opportunity. The man spoke about Anna and Håkan as if Håkan was also stuck in the snow. But that didn't necessarily mean that Håkan was at home, just that the man with the friendly voice was badly informed.

Bo didn't feel dissatisfied as he drove back along the slushy road. He felt that in some ways he had achieved a lot – even if there had been no result.

He was more concerned about the tulips until he thought of giving them to Ellen. He was a short drive away from her. That would make up for what had happened. He put on the radio but because the first thing he heard was a talk about the illnesses of old age, he quickly switched it off again. It was enough for him to hear the word 'prostate' or 'senior' to persuade him to change channel. He still had the deepest respect for medical science which had discovered that Ellen's thyroid gland was defective and replaced the hormones with something synthetic – at least he believed it was synthetic – so that she functioned like a normal person, if one could ever consider Ellen entirely normal.

As usual when she was alone, she had taken off her hearing aid and so didn't hear him coming. He stood in the hall and hung his coat up. The place looked clean and tidy. Obviously the home-help had been. Contrary to what one would expect from someone who had worked with antiques for the last forty years of her life, the little apartment was very modern and sparsely furnished. A few beautiful things, comfortable, simple and airy. Everything was patently expensive.

She was sitting near the window with the reading lamp switched on, doing a crossword. The television was switched off. It didn't even look as though she had been sitting in the chair in front of it – the cushions weren't even flattened. He was pleased about that. He thought it was awful when she sat there the whole day and used the remote control to switch from one channel to another. He wanted her to be active, not passive.

Suddenly she lifted her head and became aware of him. Then she lit up and he could see that she had taken trouble to put makeup on her face as if she were expecting someone to visit. There was rouge on her cheeks, a little too close to her ear on the right-hand side but her lipstick was perfect. Her hand had been steady and there were no fuzzy outlines. Her eyes shone when he gave her the flowers and she thanked him with a peck on the cheek. Her happiness was unaffected and almost childish. She no longer took presents for granted. After the constant complaining during convalescence it was as if she had become softer, grateful to be alive. At least that was what he imagined.

But her natural tendency to issue orders was still there. Ten minutes later he was standing meekly in the queue at the excellent pizzeria in Sybille Street. When he came back with the warm cartons she had set the table and put out a bottle. The tulips were densely packed in a ceramic jar under the lamp – pink, white, yellow and pale mauve. Several times while they were eating she stroked the petals with her fingertips and smiled at him.

'How did you know that I had been longing for tulips all day. Smell them, they remind one of spring!'

Anna woke early in the morning and realised that the sleeping tablets and painkillers had worked wonders. She could move her toes, carefully, and flex her ankles, also carefully, without getting pain in her back. Her hip was painful. But that wasn't surprising. She had been lying on the same side all night. She slowly turned onto her other side, centimetre by centimetre. It was painful but not like it had been before. Fabian got up from the foot of the bed and pressed himself into the angle between her thigh and her calf. She dare not think about how he had managed during the night. And if he hadn't managed it wasn't his fault. At that moment he was only focussed on sleeping. It was still dark outside.

Suddenly the room was lit up with a strong light and a projection of the window's six-barred panes rolled over the wall, the tall bureau and finished on the rag rug by the door. The first vehicle since the storm had passed the hilltop at the oak grove and the headlights had dipped down again. It was dark once more.

A great feeling of relief swept over her. She wasn't cut off from the world. Help was on the way. Now that it couldn't be Hilding, she hoped that it would be Anton from Tuna. The engine noise came nearer and she pictured to herself how the snow would whirl around the plough blades and how whitely it would glitter in the headlights.

It would take him a good while to get from the turning point and the avenue. In the best case he would do the forecourt as well. The engine was roaring. It almost sounded as though it was in the house. Even more snow had fallen since she had been lying there.

However that may be, she had to get up. She didn't want to be caught still in bed by Anton. She was feeling better, definitely better, but a long way from fully recovered. Before she was able to roll out of bed and get into the bathroom she was sweating with the effort and knew that she was smelling. She washed and put on the thick bathrobe. At least she was now fit to be seen by people if it was necessary. Ideally she would like to lie down again.

The tractor carried on rumbling and the plough blades scraped the ground. It sounded as if it had reached the woodshed. She could stand up and walk but not go down the stairs. The only way was to slither down the steps on her stomach and take the weight on her arms and hands. It didn't feel dignified and the bathrobe rucked up indecently. Suddenly it went quiet outside and then there was a banging on the kitchen door, which was locked. Fabian jumped over her back with a big leap and landed on the hall floor. He stood there listening. Renewed banging and he ran barking into the kitchen, while she slithered down, step by step, until her feet were on the floor. Then there was renewed ringing at the outer door's silly little bell, the one that so seldom found a use for its voice.

'Come in,' she called out and sat herself up against the wall. She called twice more before the handle of the door to the kitchen was cautiously pushed down. In the country, people happily step into the kitchen if the door is not locked, but with a heavy door it's best to be careful. One doesn't open it oneself.

It was Anton exactly as she had hoped. He stood on the doormat, big and unshaven in a draft of cold, fresh air and he looked at her in surprise.

'Back pain,' she said and hoped that it would explain everything. Beads of sweat on her forehead, hair lying loose down her back like a rat's tail, a bathrobe hanging loose on her. She pulled in the belt and tried to smile. Her lips felt as though they were glued to her teeth. Her smile must have looked like a wolf's grin.

'Oh, really,' he said, and looked hard at the floor. 'Well, now you have a clear road anyway. You can go to the doctor about your back and everything.'

'Never in a million years. But it's wonderful that you came. It was feeling a bit isolated here. Will you have some coffee?'

He would. She was sure that he had been expecting it. When he saw what difficulty she had in moving he calmly took over. His previous job was at a home for the disabled and he was experienced at looking after young people and himself. He quickly found out where things were, measured out the coffee, filled up with water and put the cups out. He found butter and cheese in the fridge, cut up the bread and then hesitated a little with his hand hovering over the marmalade jar. 'Some of that or not?' She nodded. Otherwise she just sat there relaxed and looking on.

'Where's Håkan then? Is he sleeping or something?'

'He's gone away. I have been lying here like a fallen tree completely alone. I couldn't even let Fabian out as I should have.'

'He seems to have made up for it. He stood and urinated on my tractor at least ten times,' Anton said looking out of the window. 'But you are looking very poorly. Are you sure that you shouldn't go to the doctor? You can take a taxi.'

'No. What could he do? It just takes time. In the best case a week, and then it's over.'

Anton stroked his chin and looked at her thoughtfully. Not just thoughtfully, but also a little approvingly, she imagined.

'People are very different,' he said. Ulla, Karin's mother, goes straight to the doctor if she just has a splinter in her finger. Always ready to complain. "They are paid for that," she says. Keeps on until she gets a free pass. That's status you know. Then she can go there every five minutes. For free. She sits in the waiting room or cafeteria and talks with her friends. I just don't understand it.'

Anna listened and smiled, drank her coffee in big greedy gulps and gained strength. She thought that she had never tasted such good coffee. It was hot, strong and sweet. He had scooped in the sugar with a generous hand and so she had been able to sit at her own table, without lifting a finger and be served by a big chap in his stockinged feet. She couldn't have had it better and she told him so. Otherwise the conversation was mainly about the difficulties of the last days.

There were households that had been without power for two days. And the milk cart couldn't get around. Anton wasn't the only one who was obliged to carry the milk up the hill. And the animals had no water. The farmers had to make a hole in the ice and carry it from the lake. Svennson's woodland had been damaged although it wasn't as bad as he claimed. The school bus crashed into the veterinary surgeon's car in a snow storm, but luckily no blood was spilt. There were some bruises and damage to the vehicles.

'And while we are toiling in the cold, Håkan is lying and sunning himself in the warm, I assume,' Anton said in conclusion.

Anna smiled.

'We shouldn't grudge him that. Winter is difficult for him.'

Anton gave her a quick look, as if he didn't really agree with her. Then he cleared away the cups, put them in the dishwasher and tidied up the refrigerator a bit.

'You are out of milk,' he said. 'Make a list of what you need and give it to the postwoman. They will drive out to the shops for you.'

Then he cleared the kitchen table with a damp Wettex cloth and looked around.

'I had better sweep up a bit,' he said. 'But that will be the last thing. There are other people apart from you who need help with clearing the snow.'

He stood at the door and then remembered something.

'There was someone asking after you yesterday. He told me his name but I have forgotten it.'

'What did he look like?'

Anton looked at her helplessly.

'I didn't think about it much. I was working near the church. He was just ordinary. But he had a Golf, very new. Definitely from Stockholm.'

Anna remembered a blue car at the car park on the day when Bo was out and about on the road.

'Was it blue?' she asked.

'Blue or perhaps grey. Definitely not red. I would have remembered that.'

'Was he young or old?' asked Anna, carrying on with her cross-examination.

'About your age,' he said with cautious diplomacy. 'He seemed nice but a bit worried about the state of the roads.'

She was quite sure that she knew who it was and was pleased that Bo had gone to the trouble of coming out for her sake. Grateful that he hadn't been able to reach her though. He had shown goodwill and they had avoided a meeting which would have had a doubtful outcome. Meeting someone for the first time to whom she had confided more nonsense on paper than she could remember, she didn't want to be ugly, repulsive and made stupid and dull by tablets. She wanted at least to look worth making the journey for.

'The telephone is still not functioning. It will probably take a few more days. We out here are being de-prioritised for everything,' Anton said, giving Anna a new buzzword to think about before he left.

The thought that Bo might come back frightened her into the shower room. She had to wash her hair if she died in the attempt. Fortunately there were clean clothes in a heap next to the ironing board in the laundry room. She didn't have to get up the stairs to the bedroom in order to be decently clothed. But she would keep her bathrobe on over everything else because she felt frozen from sheer misery.

Much later the postwoman's van was standing outside the kitchen door, which was now kept permanently unlocked. She needed to look out for the old and infirm when the telephone was playing up. Anton had obviously thought that Anna qualified for that group and had summoned help. The postwoman called out and stepped straight into the kitchen, fresh and rosy-cheeked. She laid the post on the kitchen table.

Then she stood by the kitchen sofa where Anna was lying on her back with her knees draw up and her calves resting against an empty beer carton with a cushion on top.

'You are alone here then,' she said. 'I heard that the old chap isn't at home to look after you. Is there anything you want from the shops?'

Anna had already prepared a list. Skimmed milk, oranges, sliced cheese, some fresh greens, slices of ham and some Marabou milk chocolate.

'I'll bring them with me tomorrow if the shop doesn't make a delivery themselves before then,' she promised. 'And I will look in on you in any case.'

As soon as she was out of the door, Anna got up and dragged herself to the kitchen table. When the postwoman had come in, she had brought with her a thick brown envelope. And as they were talking Anna had guessed what the contents were. All of her letters, which Bo was sending back after yesterday's journey into her wilderness. He must have realised how impossible a meeting was and how even more impossible it was for them to continue. He came, he saw and turned back. For good, it seemed. The old feeling of despair she had experienced at school dances rose up from forgotten depths. Not worth it. No good. The men in her vicinity didn't want to know her. They were struck dumb, ran away, cut off all ties.

But when she had put on her glasses she saw that it wasn't Bo's writing on the envelope but Lasse's. It was true that there was a resemblance but she couldn't understand how she could have mistaken her own son's handwriting and was ashamed of her foolishness. He had taped up the envelope rather liberally and she cut it open with the bread knife and took out a bundle of photos. Lasse had obviously wanted to cheer up Grandpa and Grandma with photos of the grandchildren. Simon and pale Emma were impartially shown, perhaps with some predominance of shots of Simon. He was after all their own grandson and therefore closer to her heart – and Lasse knew that. The stepchild had her own grandmother within walking distance.

Anna had noticed that the greater the distance between her and Lasse in terms of time and space, the more photos he sent to compensate. Letter writing had never been his thing. She had heard it said that a picture tells more than a hundred words. On the telephone he was terse. Like his father he thought that it was for messages, not small talk. But he certainly rang frequently. He was kind, her Lasse. She herself seldom rang. Partly because she most often only got the answering machine, and partly because Lasse shouldn't have to put his head in his hands and say: 'Oh, no! Mother again. What does she want now!'

She had decided that she didn't want to stick to her son like a postage stamp. Or to his partner. They shouldn't have to groan about her.

She looked at the photos that had just arrived. The family had obviously been on an outing to a zoo during the autumn. There were pictures of the children cuddling goats and sheep and sitting on ponies. Then there were winter pictures. They seemed to have had plenty of snow. They were on snow saucers, sledges and sleighs. There was a photo of Simon half-buried in the snow with his very short skis poking into the air. He was laughing and had snow all over his head. She liked that one and put it up on the notice board in the kitchen.

She wondered if Lasse imagined that his parents bent over the photos together and pointed to the youngsters with loving smiles. He probably did. Lasse was very uncomplicated. He still wished that she and Håkan lived nearer. He declared that they would be really good grandparents. He thought that he had had an excellent childhood. It was a good thing he thought so. It would never have occurred to him to discuss all of childhoods bitter disappointments with her, even less so with Håkan. In that way he and Malin were very different.

However, even he understood that it required a certain geographic proximity for grandparental affection to blossom. That was why he sent so many photos. Her conscience pricked her and she went through the bundle again and found a picture of Emma where she was laughing together with Simon. They looked as though they were ready to eat each other up. That also went up on the board so that Emma wouldn't be hurt, although deep in her heart she knew that the girl could be mean to Simon. She was more quick-witted and good at manipulating her surroundings. She didn't actually deserve to be on the board.

Håkan thought that the youngsters were unattractive. One could see it from the way he looked at the pictures with raised eyebrows and a turned down mouth as if he could not understand how those children could have anything to do with him.

It was the flash-lights that made them look so staring and pale in the face, she explained to him. But if she was honest, she didn't think they were particularly sweet either. Emma's little lips were thin and Simon was no oil painting. His eyelashes were pale and his eyes light blue.

As soon as she had those thoughts, her conscience pricked her. A grandmother shouldn't think like that. Grandmothers should be full of love and completely uncritical. She wasn't a good example. She knew that those children weren't in a particularly good situation. She should have hurried to the rescue. But she neither could nor would. She sent books when she remembered, and was near a bookshop. And sometimes a funny card, which she spent a long time carefully choosing. She didn't know if any adult would take the time to read the books out loud to them, least of all Lasse although perhaps he would. He wanted to be a good father. But she couldn't see Carina sitting on the side of the bed and reading bedtime stories. There were cassettes for that.

She should be happy that she was remembered and received all these photos, seeing how little joy she spread around to her children and grandchildren. Carina's mother pasted every photo into an album and documented them for her daughter and herself. Carina took it for granted that her mother-in-law was equally dutiful. Every year she gave Anna a new album to put the new photos in. They lay unopened in a cupboard with the photos next to them in a wooden box. It would soon be full. Her fear was that Carina would want to look at the albums the next time she came for a visit. How would Anna explain that she hasn't been able to stick in a single photo?

She had not been able to persuade herself to bring some order into the family photos of the last thirty years. She had tried to interest Håkan in the photo album project but why should he be able to face up to old memories when she couldn't? The idea was stillborn from the beginning. It would be completely unreasonable to expect any such thing from him. Even the sweetest photos can be terribly upsetting in retrospect.

Nevertheless they'd been happy – in their way – happy and content enough for a while, particularly during the years when the children were small, before they began school. And even later. Even as recently as Tuesday when they skied together in a small pale stretch of contentment.

But she was sure of one thing: that she and Håkan were the poorer for not having had Simon – and Emma – nearer to them. Happiness at being able to be with the grandchildren and see them on weekdays without exorbitant expectations on both sides had eluded them. It wasn't anyone's fault. It was just something that happened. But as things were now, they had to get used to each all over again each time they met. There was always the same tentative beginning before they could start to trust one another. Then it was time to leave.

Perhaps Håkan would have felt good about having grandchildren nearby to be interested in. Strict fathers who hadn't had much time for their own children, often became devoted grandmothers and grandfathers. They lapped up what used to be called 'life's dessert'. But that was obviously only speculation. Probably she and Håkan were already so fixed in their ways that it was best as it was.

But she had friends – Gertrud was one of them and obviously Bo was also – who almost every day picked up children from kindergarten, drove them to ballet, accompanied them to riding and ice hockey, took them to museums and invited them to McDonald's. They were tired but needed. That was enviable – very enviable. But constant contact with children and grandchildren is not something one gets for free.

She and Håkan also had friends – Gertrud was one of them and she suspected that Bo might do the same – who still had their wedding photo in a silver frame, standing on view in a place of honour, often with a light or a flower next to it. The thought that she and Håkan would have theirs on view – if they even had one – was dizzying. Neither of them could have put up with a daily reminder of how wrong it had gone.

When she was younger and more robust she smiled at those photos in all their splendour, retouched and time-bound. She thought them very bourgeois. Now she was almost touched when she saw those young couples, her in a veil and headdress, him in uniform as was usually the case during and after the war. Now she saw those photos as evidence that the couple had lived and continued to live in a good and strong marriage. No one had, in a fit of anger thrown the photo against a slammed door. No glass had splintered, no cardboard backing had been torn. No one had stamped on it in rage until it crunched under their soles. The wedding photographs in their silver frames stood there solemnly through the decades. Bride and bridegroom look at each other seriously. They didn't have much idea but they knew that they shouldn't be roaring with laughter like modern newlyweds in the newspapers. And it went well with them in life. They had stuck together through crises and were still fine together.

That could make her envious. If she and Håkan had had a wedding photo perhaps things would have been better for them, been more dignified. But she was the kind of girl who wasn't suited to be standing there as a bride in a veil and train. She didn't have it in her like her sisters did.

Suddenly it was as if she could see herself in a blinding light, sitting at her kitchen table. A disappointed and envious old woman. She was seventy-two years old, almost seventy-three, and hadn't achieved any order in her life. Her husband had just got up and left. Her children had chosen to live so far away that they hardly needed to meet her. She had even looked belatedly for some comfort by advertising in the Personal column for a man. And now that man seemed as frightened by the venture as she was. He would probably not appear again.

To live so long and achieve so little. There was failure all around wherever she looked. Not even Fabian was exactly what she wanted. Sometimes he threw a cheeky look at her and ran away. Then she could stand there and shout for him to no avail.

'But at least I am hard-working,' she said to the empty air. 'I don't waste my days.'

Restless, she inwardly answered herself. Frightened of my own thoughts and not daring to sit and think. Having to be on the move all the time and fiddling with one thing or another, just to avoid seeing my life as it is. And what about Håkan's.

How can it have gone so wrong?

De-prioritised was definitely the right word. The telephone wasn't working the next day either. She thought that perhaps the mobile phones she despised had their uses after all. But even if she had a telephone, she didn't have any great desire to speak to anyone. As far as Håkan was concerned she was if anything grateful for every day in which she was spared the conversation she might have had with him. Sooner or later he would surface again. Probably in a bad state. She was sure of that.

She had a greetings card with a picture of a yellow-haired, rosy-cheeked angel, which she had intended for Emma. She sent it to Bo instead. 'Thank you for the greetings. The roads are passable again but I am suffering from back pain. Lunch will have to wait,' she wrote.

Simon should have received the *Emil i Lönneberg* card but she sent that to her sister Agneta instead. 'Everything is all right, but the telephone is not working. We will speak later.' It wasn't that she or Agneta would be worried if they didn't hear from one another but she thought that the card addressed to Bo would catch the eye less if it had feminine company while it was lying waiting on the kitchen table. Common sense told her that the postwoman would certainly have other things to think about than who was writing to whom, but it felt to Anna as though she was positively putting on display her secret plans for a late romance. A least that was what she feared.

In exchange for the cards to be mailed, she received the day's post and a bag of goods from the shop. The oranges were old and the leeks were yellow and drooping but the milk and ham hadn't passed their best-before date. As soon as she was alone, she leafed through the envelopes. There was a bill from Statoil, two letters from Handelsbank – banks squandered envelopes dreadfully – and one from Bo. She opened it.

Dear Anna,

Have tried in vain to phone you. Drove out to you, but nothing came of it. A yeoman on a tractor assured me you were alive. If I don't hear anything from you, I will come back. You don't have to let me in, just let me know if I can help. For example, by shovelling snow or cutting wood.

Affectionately Bo.

★

He had never written 'Affectionately' before. It touched her a little. And he was ready to make the journey in spite of the risk of possibly meeting Håkan. That touched her even more. She was unstable and soppy, a grateful object of charity. Tears ran for no reason. She was about to come loose at the joints. She blew her nose and it sounded loud in the silence. Then she tried the telephone. It was as dead as ever.

For the rest of the day she dozed in her bed or listened to

the radio from time to time and then quickly turned it off. As soon as she woke up she continued thinking endlessly about her life and also conducted long imaginary conversations, sometimes with Håkan and sometimes with Bo. They were fuzzy in outline but still engrossing. She brooded about Malin and why she had chosen the life she had. Because in spite of her successful career, there was still something careless about the way she lived. She had been an impulsive and anxious teenager, unbelievably energetic but very angry and certainly not orderly. She continued to strew things around whenever she came to visit. Hadn't changed at all in that respect. But she liked children, was still able to get even sly little Emma to gasp with laughter, yet didn't want her own. As a girl she had always been surrounded by boys, never had a girl as her best friend. It was still men who mattered most to her, but she didn't want a husband or family. She was impossible to understand. Still, Anna had not been the kind of mother Malin could identify with.

The childhood she and Håkan had given their daughter must somehow have been a deterrent to building a family. But they had done the best they could. There was a lot that should not have been done. The thought of all those failures was difficult to bear. She crawled round and rolled out of the bed to take a distalgesic to deaden the pain.

But her troubling thoughts about Malin delayed its effect for quite a while. Anna longed for her with a sudden intensity. In the old days they had sat together half the night and talked. They had found it easy. But that was a long time ago and she wondered what she had done that made Malin so reluctant to come home. She would like so much to sit and talk to her again and to find out what kind of person she had become.

★

At nightfall – just when she had forced herself to go down to the kitchen and put together something to eat – she saw in the dark the headlights of a car on the road. It couldn't be Bo. He would never have come so late. She quickly took the frying pan off before the lump of butter burned. From the window she could see the cones of light approaching at speed. It struck her that it could be Håkan in an extravagant limousine hired in Arlanda and thinking of making a big entrance with a clinking purse in his hand. He had done that before. Her whole body stiffened and she resisted the idea. Not yet, not yet.

The headlights swept right into the kitchen when the car turned up towards the forecourt. She held her breath and stood motionless, defenceless in the face of unknown dangers. The doors were unlocked, anyone could come straight in and strike her down. She didn't have any time to escape. And Fabian had no idea what a protective instinct was. He wagged his tail, expectant and bright-eyed.

Outside by the car someone was getting his things together from the back seat with his back towards her. Then he turned round and waved. Then she realised that it was Lasse! She hadn't even recognised his neck and back, had thought that it was a robber or attacker. But in the midst of her joy she felt a stab of disappointment in her heart. Then she was ashamed. At her age she ought to rank her son higher than an old archivist she had never even met.

Then she felt Lasse's beard against her cheek – less rough than one would think but unexpected. She would never get used to it. It didn't suit him. He was dressed in an unusual mixture of fox red and brown. That was obviously Carina's influence. It showed something but she didn't know what.

But at the same time there was something attractive about the beard in its close-cropped and well-groomed colourfulness. She rubbed her cheek against it and felt his strong warm hands on her shoulders. For a short while she allowed herself to be taken care of and protected, then she peered into his face with a mother's instinctive preparedness for catastrophes.

'Is there something wrong? With the children or Carina?'

'Relax. There's nothing wrong with us. It was you we were worried about, with all this snow and the telephone not working. Believe it or not, but Malin was worried when she couldn't get through even though she kept trying for two days. We agreed that I should come out and look at you. By the way you are looking very peaky... peaky and thin.'

That was not perhaps exactly what she wanted to hear but she was still touched by their thoughtfulness. Malin didn't usually get worried and Lasse certainly wasn't someone who worked himself up unnecessarily. Quite the opposite. It was a mystery to her how she could have produced a son who even under the most chaotic of circumstances was always convinced that everything would turn out for the best. But it was difficult for her to believe that he had really driven thirty miles to make sure that she was alive. He was obviously on some other errand as well. That would all come out in good time.

'It's nothing!' she said. 'I'm not feeling so peaky anymore but I have back pain so I have been lying down almost all day. That's why I am slouching around in a dressing-gown.'

'That's what we thought. That something was wrong.' He looked at her enquiringly with concern in his eyes. That melted her heart. It really melted it, so that she felt quite soft inside. It was so long since anyone in the family had looked at all concerned for her. She felt tears coming into her eyes and blinked them away. Apparently she could no longer cope with normal kindness.

'Have you heard from Papa?'

She looked at him in surprise. How did he know that Håkan was away?

'Malin received a picture postcard a few days ago. From Madeira. He seemed happy. But we assumed that. I am starving.'

Lasse sniffed the air for a moment with a contented look on his face. It smelt like melted butter and that's what it was. She had been standing at the stove with the frying-pan ready just as he came through the door. Preparing food for the children in one of a mother's most important tasks. And it makes the children happy.

'I was thinking of making an omelette for myself. If that's not enough for you, you can look in the fridge and find something you would like.'

He poked about among the packages and found a packet of bubble and squeak. Then he muttered a bit about how she still didn't have a microwave oven. That she didn't realise how convenient it would be.

'But I'm never in a hurry. At my age one isn't in a hurry when preparing a meal.'

'But still. It saves power as well. You really should.'

It was strange what trivial and uninteresting things they spoke about and disagreed about during the first minutes when she and the children met. She thought that it was because they saw each other so seldom that they had to speak about trivial things while they got used to one another. She knew what Lasse was thinking. She had become so old, so haggard and so neglected, but still as touchy as ever. She couldn't take any advice, always thought that she knew best.

On her part she thought he had put on weight since she last saw him. The boyish look had disappeared. He looked like a man now. Perhaps it was the beard. Or perhaps not. She still wasn't sure what she thought about it. And while she was thinking about that she asked after Carina and the grandchildren. Was Simon happier with the new child-minder? And thank you for the photos. Feeling very pleased with herself, she pointed to the kitchen noticeboard where the pictures of both Simon and Emma were pinned up. It was so very lucky that she had put them there where they could be seen so quickly.

'Not exactly brilliant photos, no flash,' said Lasse.

But nevertheless he looked pleased. She had behaved like a real grandmother.

She chopped up an onion to give some extra flavour to the bubble and squeak, found some pickled beetroot in the fridge and put an extra knob of butter in the frying pan before choosing the two largest eggs in the box. It was the age-old custom of trying to show her love with something good and beneficial in the absence of the right spontaneous word. It was as if she hoped that the small talk would cease if she took a short cut straight to his stomach.

'Shall we open a bottle of wine. To celebrate?'

But that didn't suit at all. Lasse had to get up early the next morning. He also didn't think they had much to celebrate with Håkan on the wrong road.

Then she got angry. As if anxiety should be a reason to abstain from wine when it was rather the opposite. This was obviously something Carina had instigated in her petty-bourgeois way.

'Goodness me,' she said, 'it's not the first time Håkan has taken himself off. I don't understand why you are suddenly getting upset about it. It never used to bother you, neither you nor Malin. In any case I'm going to have a glass.'

'He is older now. An old man. It's pathetic. You must see that? It's nothing to get angry about, but still he shouldn't gad about just as he pleases.

'Why not if that's what he wants to do?'

They looked hard at each other without anyone giving way. It was almost like his brief moments of teenage rebellion. The one who stares longest and most vacantly wins. But they were both too old for such games.

'Sometimes it feels as if you, and Malin too, barely make it through the door before you find fault with me. I can't bear it. I know that you think that I am so mean to your poor old papa that he can't stand being at home. But it's not like that.'

He shook his head and looked at her, sighed over her silliness and finally took her by the shoulders. Then she relaxed.

'If I had known how it was for you here in the snow, I would have come sooner,' he said. 'You should have told us as soon as he left!'

'I like being on my own,' she protested. 'Usually I enjoy it. But the back pain took away some of the pleasure this time. Your papa will be all right in any case. You don't need to worry about him. He was unusually spry when he left.'

Lasse opened up the wine bottle in a moment of reconciliation and filled the glasses while she served up a large portion of bubble and squeak for him and a smaller one for herself. She would eat the omelette when she was alone again.

'What had he written on the card to Malin?'

He looked a bit embarrassed and waved his hands as if to distance himself from it.

"Här var det livat, här var det glatt, här var det blommor i morsans hatt."[28]

They looked at each other, then Anna snorted. That was so crazy. The Håkan she knew for almost half a century would never have expressed himself in that way. He didn't know any doggerel, not a single nursery-rhyme, not even the words to any ancient hit song. He had no use for such a thing. But now apparently something had floated up from his inner reserves. It was not particularly impressive.

But that was also something she recognised. Once again he had cut the moorings to the ravaged shore of reality. Now nothing was impossible for him. He was no longer the pensioned-off provincial lawyer with a scandal-ridden reputation. He was lovable gentleman with a way with women – the person he'd always known he was deep down. At the moment he was filled with confidence. It was when he landed back in ever day life again that things would become difficult.

'He is obviously in high spirits,' Anna observed drily.

'But it's getting out of hand. He's stark raving mad! Have you checked money, plastic cards and the like? How long ago was it that he ran away?'

She was ashamed that she could not be precise. It looked as though she didn't care.

'It came quite unexpectedly. For him as well, I'm sure of that,' she said defensively.

Suddenly she felt the desire to talk. It was rare that one of the children was at home and listening to her. She twisted the wine glass between her fingers and gave her son a searching look as if she wondered how much cold fact he could handle.

Then she painted with a flowing brush the scene in the courtyard when Hilde Apeldoorn had sat waiting for their return in her red car. Anna hadn't forgotten a single detail: the slits in the black cape, the peacock blue silk sleeves. Håkan's expression too – half-delighted and half-ashamed, but also how his delight increased. And even how he had introduced her, Anna, as his elder sister.

Lasse listened with his eyes riveted on her, at once spellbound and incredulous, just as he had been when he was little and she told him fairy stories. Against his will he was moved.

'But how could you let him go like that,' he said at last. 'With a total stranger?'

'She wasn't a stranger to him,' she pointed out. 'They had met before and made plans, though whether he had rooted for it in some way or she surprised him wasn't clear to me.'

'I don't understand how he can have planned a meeting with a foreign woman with you close by. You are always together. He doesn't have a telephone in his room.'

'I am not his gaoler. I don't open his post and I don't listen to his telephone calls, for the simple reason that he never speaks on the telephone when I am in the house. But I don't stick to him like glue. I move around. If he wants to call someone, he can do it without my knowing it. There is only one thing that's unusual this time: he hasn't left an address. He has cut the umbilical cord. Previously he's always ensured that I would be able to rescue him if he got into trouble. But there's nothing to worry about. He has a guardian angel. He's always succeeded in getting home so far. He's protected.'

She could almost see him in front of her, there in the sun. It was easy, because during the course of the years she had seen many photos of him taken by casual acquaintances, mostly at some open-air restaurant. There he would be sitting with a drink in one hand and an English newspaper spread out in front of him. He'd be wearing shorts with his brown legs stretched out under the table. They were surprisingly well preserved. No knots of blue veins. He liked to wear thin light woollen socks and well brushed leather shoes. He had never cared for sandals. They didn't suit his image – the perfect gentleman in his short-sleeved tennis shirt with a thin grey pullover carelessly slung over his shoulders. His hair was bleached by water and sun to a shining silver. A tan smoothed out the lines and wrinkles and behind the sunglasses one could divine a lightly ironic smile. All that lawyerly stiffness and solemnity at work was contrived. He liked to think he looked like a public-school Englishman. He was fixated on that image of himself, and always reverted to it when he left ordinary life behind him. That lifelong piece of deception made him feel secure and relaxed.

As he sat there, slim and tanned, he was a magnet for older women on the lookout. Distinguished-looking and with something about him that signalled he was open to offers. There had been times when Anna had hoped that someone would want to look after him permanently. If she had only felt that he would manage reasonably well, she would gladly have released him. She'd begrudge him getting a better lifestyle, because she didn't think he deserved it, but if he met a kind wealthy widow or divorced woman…

'Perhaps it is strange that he can still attract women,' she said. 'On ordinary days he's hardly a big shot, and of course as dumb as a fish.'

Lasse snorted contemptuously.

'He travels to these holiday places. What do you expect?

Attracting women there is no great skill and he has always been able to do it – including the time he was left half-dead and lying in hospital after that car accident. There was still a pretty nurse sitting on his bed when Malin and I trotted in to visit him during our breakfast break. How angry we were. And shocked. We went in there expecting to feel sorry for him and there he lay, pawing a nurse.'

'Yes, yes,' said Anna. 'That's over and done with long ago. You know what he's like and it's not something to get excited about. I don't understand why you're getting so worked up. We're not senile. He is a bit crazy, true, but he has been for a long time. He doesn't wander around unable to take care of himself, like they say on the radios notifications about missing persons.'

'But don't you realise that it could be dangerous if he gets wound up? People die in situations like that.'

'If you think I am being irresponsible you can ring the Dutch seductress. Her number is on the board, in the right-hand corner. Yes, just there,' she said when Lasse removed the note with the number in Holland.

Anna had forgotten about his mobile-phone, which was lying charged up in his briefcase. She hadn't realised with that at the kitchen table they were no longer cut off from the world. His smug smile was annoying as he began to tap in the number.

'I am not going to speak to her,' Anna said firmly.

Lasse continued putting in the number but as soon as the ringing started, held out the telephone to her. She refused to take it. Then he laid it on the table in front of her, got up and stood at the window with his back to her.

Perhaps she wasn't at home! Anna screwed up her eyes

to concentrate all her will-power on that thought. But Hilda Apeldoorn answered with her surname and it only required Anna to put the phone to her ear and say her piece. Lasse's back was motionless as he listened.

'Oh, dear,' said Hilda in her good English. Had Håkan really not been in touch? She had reminded him several times. He was a bad boy, wasn't he! But there was nothing to worry about. He was feeling really good as recently as Thursday when they parted at the airport. He wanted to stay for another week. If Anna could just wait, Hilde would fetch the address and telephone number of the hotel. It was no problem at all.

It was definitely the first time in more than twenty-five years that Anna had spoken to one of Håkan's women. She'd always thought of herself as above that. It was even longer since she had stopped checking up on him. Now she didn't bother getting emotional. Hilde obviously felt put on the spot but Anna but didn't care about that. She was convinced that Hilde no longer thought that she was his elder sister. She could hear that in the lightly complicitous tone. There was also something condescending in the way she repeated the address and telephone number of the hotel twice, as if she thought that Anna might have difficulty in hearing or understanding. On the other hand, she complained that Håkan hadn't written to her even though she'd pressed him to. She seemed to have assumed all the rights of a wife, including nagging. Anna concluded this annoying conversation curtly.

'I didn't remember how snooty you can sound,' said Lasse from the window.

It was difficult to know whether he meant it as praise or criticism.

'Here's the number for the hotel. I'm not calling it. I have done enough. It was your idea and your telephone. You can do it yourself if you are so worried. Which I find difficult to believe.'

The conversation that followed was complicated and full of linguistic misunderstandings. Apparently there was no English-speaking person available at the hotel. It was unclear whether Håkan had already checked out or was just not answering from his room. Lasse wasn't sure that he and the concierge were talking about the same person. For Anna it was as if a pastiche of *Fawlty Towers* was being played out in her kitchen.

'I am from Barcelona. I know nothing,' she said and waved her arms when Lasse put down the receiver. He looked blankly at her and shook his head.

Obviously he didn't sit slumped in front of old television repeats like his elderly parents. They had different terms of reference now and anything else would have been strange. But she missed those times when there had been only one or two TV channels. Then it was much easier to maintain a shared view of the world. She had a measure of control. They'd laughed about the same things, she and the children.

'I'll see if I can get hold of him in the morning and let you know,' Lasse said. But it sounded as though the fire had gone out of him. He wouldn't ring again.

'How can you let me know when I'm without a telephone?'

Lasse shrugged his shoulders. It would sort itself out. Håkan was obviously at that hotel he liked in Madeira and the most important thing was that they had tracked him down. It sounded as though her son thought that the problem had been solved. And that was more like him.

While she sat drinking her coffee, Lasse made two more calls. Once to Malin, or rather to her answering machine to say Papa had been tracked down. Everything was OK. Mamma was fine but still without a telephone.

The other call was to Carina. Anna listened hard while standing at the kitchen sink. She tried to take the temperature of their marriage from the tone of his voice. She sometimes had her doubts. Standing in his mother's kitchen, he knew that she was listening. His voice sounded somewhere between neutral and warm. He was just ringing to check that everything was all right at home. Obviously, it was. She noticed that he didn't say anything about Håkan and wondered if he kept Carina out of the loop on family problems. If he was ashamed of his parents. It mostly sounded as if the meeting in Stockholm was the most important reason for his journey, and the overnight visit to her a secondary matter, a small diversion on the way.

Which was precisely what Anna had suspected.

When he finished the conversation, he went over to her where she was standing by the coffee percolator. She was tall but he was taller. He had to bend closer when he said, 'What do you think about becoming a grandmother again towards the summer?'

It came so suddenly and unexpectedly that she could only look at him. Then she felt a spurt of joy. Now *that* was unexpected. To be so happy that Lasse and Carina were having a child. To be so happy! It must be the primordial power of a woman's soul that rejoiced in a new life, because the mind doesn't really do that.

But a primordial power does it.

★

It was a clear morning with a crescent moon in the west and a rosy red sky in the east when Lasse left. She stood at the window and waved at the car as she always did when the children left. It was possible that Lasse thought that she wiped away a sad tear, but already she was thinking about something else. A quiet expectation was rising inside her – she was quite sure that Bo would appear at some time during the day.

She sat rigidly at the kitchen table. Her back hadn't been made worse from Lasse's visit, but better. Or perhaps she hadn't had time to notice it. There was still some warm coffee in the percolator and she drank slowly with both hands around the cup and her elbows resting on the table. She thought about the new little life, which would continue well into the next century, and how very pleased she was about it. Yet it had never seemed to her that the parents-to-be had time, or made time, for the two children they had already, so why should they be any more suited to raising the new one? She defended herself a bit for suspecting that the child's arrival was a hopeful manoeuvre to mend a half-broken marriage and bind the family together. It was not right to place such expectations on the poor unborn baby.

Her own little dead one didn't even get the chance to try.

She sighed a bit and the house echoed around her. A few moments ago she had heard Lasse's voice from the bedroom. He was lively in the morning and talked while he got up. Håkan was the same once upon a time. Strange how small habits recur in families.

His visit had livened her up in spite of all the unnecessary nonsense about Håkan. She found it difficult to understand the children's concern for him. It had come about so recently and was perhaps intended mostly to heap glowing coals on her head.

The coffee was finished and it was time to get a grip on life again; to put clothes on her back and to see if it was reasonably clear in the kitchen. But she remained sitting at the table. Something was trying to get her attention and be looked at from all sides, but she didn't know what it was. Something altogether different had taken up her thoughts – Lasse, Håkan, the news about the new little life and Bo's possible visit. She wasn't used to having so much to think about. But she knew that something had woken her up during the night and made her think that there was something she had to take in hand in the morning. Probably a dream that had disappeared in the way that dreams do. Nothing for her to worry about.

There was also something else that she should do but didn't want to. She reluctantly got up and laid herself cautiously on her back with bent knees and her feet firmly on the kitchen floor. It was hard, uncomfortable and, not surprisingly, quite dirty. The purpose of the manoeuvre was that with her hands folded on her chest she would lift her spine and the small of her back as high as she could, twenty-five times at a stretch without resting. It was an infallible method of strengthening the back. It had been Gertrud – in her role of doctor's wife – who had taught her the exercise it and it helped. But it was not a pleasure.

She was just doing her seventeenth lift when the telephone rang piercingly through the kitchen for the first time in several days. It rang several times before she finally managed to get up and lift the receiver.

'Why are you out of breath,' asked Gertrud. 'Are you ill?'

'No. I rushed to get here in time,' lied Anna, who wanted to keep her back-pain to herself without a lot of good advice from Gertrud. 'I didn't know that the telephone was working. You are the first to get through.'

'You have no idea how worried I was about you. Firstly, I received a cryptic card from Håkan, and then your telephone wasn't working. You could have been lying there dead without anyone knowing about it. You must get one of those mobile phones as soon as you can. I rang both Agneta and Lasse but neither had heard a sound from you. I am really annoyed with Lasse. It is indefensible that he doesn't check up on his mother. He didn't seem to know much about Håkan either for that matter.

'But Lasse was here over-night. He left only about an hour ago.'

'Then it's just as well I clearly frightened him a bit,' said Gertrud with satisfaction.

Anna swallowed. She had lost some of the pleasure she had taken in the visit – her son had been frightened into it by Gertrud, combined with his own concern for Håkan and apparently cheered on by Malin. He'd also been paid handsomely thanks to reimbursements and travel allowances. And to think she had been a bit moved by his concern!

'What did Håkan have to say on the card?' she asked.

Gertrud cleared her throat to gain a bit of time.

'It was from Arlanda. A bit peculiar. "A man is as old as he feels. H." It can't be anyone but him writing to me, can it?'

'Hardly. Does he usually write to you when he is away?'

'Never, as far as I can remember. Perhaps he saw me at the opera and thought of the old days. Or of his age.'

'It's impossible to know what he thought or didn't think.

In any case he is in Madeira now and is staying a while longer.'

'With the witch?'

'No, no. That is already a thing of the past. He is on his own.'

Whether Gertrud was disappointed with that development was not clear. She responded only by saying that in her opinion Madeira was an unusually boring island, although of course it depended on where you were staying and with whom you associated. But that wasn't what she was ringing about. She wanted to entice Anna into town, saying they could go to the theatre. She had tickets. And Anna should take the opportunity to get out while she didn't have Håkan to take into account.

It was an attractive offer, but not so attractive that Anna accepted. Instead she pleaded too much work. Although it was a lame excuse that Gertrud couldn't accept. She had been happily and well pensioned off for a long time. All talk of professional commitments she took for boasting about superior mental vitality.

'Isn't it time that you gave a young person the possibility of earning a living now that it is so hard for them to find a job? You must have done your bit by now and no one is irreplaceable. It's not as though you are on your uppers.'

It was a completely unsatisfactory conversation which left an unpleasant after-taste. Gertrud was hurt and Anna was left pondering. Did Gertrud really think that it was time for her to give up, that she was no longer capable of doing satisfactory work?

She was just beginning to put things away in the kitchen when the phone rang again. This time it was Agneta. They were on the attack this morning, her old class-mate and her sister.

'Gertrud rang yesterday and was absolutely awful,' said Agneta. She was sure that you were dying while covered in blood, having been struck down by robbers. She almost managed to convince me to believe it as well. Then she immediately tried to force me to drive all the way to your house to set about the robbers. And when I absolutely couldn't because I had an appointment at the hospital, she thought that Hugo should do it. Hugo, with his bad leg and his crutches! And he can't see much either because of his cataracts.'

'She means well but she is becoming a caricature of herself. It comes to us all in time.'

'Yes, it certainly does. Yesterday I put a carton of milk into the dishwasher instead of the fridge. The dishes turned out as shiny as if they had been polished. I've never done that before.'

'Oh, these things happen but there is nothing wrong with you. Be careful when you go out with the dog though. See that you don't fall.'

Agneta promised and Anna saw her in front of her very clearly for a brief moment. The thick curly white hair, the lively little face with its fine network of lines on the cheeks. She was still sweet, her sister. But she was six years older, six years nearer absolute old age. Anna was suddenly filled with affection for her. She couldn't imagine life without Agneta. She had always been there and they belonged together. But still they didn't often meet. The main thing was that she existed and that they remembered the same things, even if from a different perspective and in a different light. She also had the happy ability of making sorrows and disasters seem less severe and catastrophic than they were. That had been a help on many occasions.

While Anna was in the shower she thought she heard the

telephone ring. Naked, with wet slippery feet and with a towel trailing behind her she rushed to answer it. But it was too late. Bo – if it was him – had given up. She stood there with the receiver in one hand and the towel in the other, covering her chest and stomach for decency, and waited for a while. But he remained gone and she was actually grateful. It would have felt really inappropriate to have spoken to him in that state.

The next time it rang she had her bathrobe on and answered cautiously, suddenly very shy and hesitant. But it was Anticimex offering her a new advantageous insurance against pests. She could avoid all problems with mice, rats, wasps, ants, beetles and grubs in general.

Summer, with its wasps and ants seemed very remote. It was minus eight degrees outside and the snow was lying around in high drifts. Fabian was freezing on the veranda waiting to be let in. When she opened the door for him the winter followed him in, crept under her bathrobe and cooled her bare legs.

The time had gone strangely fast, perhaps because she did everything so slowly. It was already past ten o'clock. Bo definitely couldn't arrive yet – if he came at all. If he expected lunch then she was ready for that. There were lamb cutlets and butter-fried mixed mushrooms in the freezer. There were home-grown sugar snaps from the garden plus frozen potato wedges from Findus. There was also wine. They wouldn't run the risk of finding it difficult to converse because of an empty stomach and being sober. If he didn't drink because he was driving a car it would be a pity for both of them. But she hoped and believed that he would have a small glass. In such a situation.

Because she might be subject to inspection, she made an

extra effort. The days of back pain hadn't improved her looks. A little rouge and powder could work wonders but she had no illusions. She had been here before. She knew how it ended, because she never went to the Karlsberg ball.[29] Harriet and Agneta were invited several times and swept up the palace steps in long dresses with bare shoulders and borrowed fur capes, while the younger students sighed appreciatively. She was never invited.

No matter how old she grew, Anna never seemed to be able to get rid of that disappointed girl inside her. The one who never really measured up. It was morbid. Pitiful. Contemptible.

She straightened up when she stood in front of the mirror and tried to smile. It didn't make things much better, but at least she wouldn't have lipstick on her front teeth. She did her hair carefully. It was as if all the store of femininity she might still have was located there. She brushed the curly neck-length hair and pinned it up, while thinking about the last time she'd received a kiss on the neck. It was many years ago and it wasn't from Håkan. It must have been Bengt, Gertrud's Bengt, in the dining-room next to the kitchen of their villa after a very good dinner. 'You didn't know that, did you Gertrud?' she thought with a certain relish.

Then suddenly the forgotten dream came back to her. She who seldom had a dream worth remembering, had had a really splendid one. She was young in the dream and wearing some kind of ballet dress of light-blue tulle; she was slim and lithe with long tanned legs, and light as a feather. That was already surprising. She had been slim and had brown legs, but she had never been graceful. She had always been the troll, while the other little girls floated by as fairies.

In the dream she was balancing, with her head poised

gracefully, on a narrow bar set high above the ground. Håkan walked below her – young and handsome in dainty silk trousers like a 17th century cavalier – and supported her lightly with uplifted arms. His touch filled her with confidence. She danced from her bar, which had no resemblance to those in her school gym that she so often fell from as a girl. It was a moment of complete happiness. The intimacy of this dream was so strong that she'd hardly experienced anything like it in reality. And least of all in her marriage.

It was wishful thinking of course. Who wouldn't want to soar high above the hard ground, borne up by tenderness? Who wouldn't want to be as light as a feather with thin brown thighs?

Such a beautiful and incredibly clear dream must have contained a message. It must have been something beyond a nostalgic dream of youth and love and perfect balance. Perhaps she should see it as a harbinger of better times. She and Håkan might jointly be able to cope with the last stage of life together, if they held together and trusted one another.

But in that case, it would be only right that he too had such a dream to give him something to think about. Preferably every night so that the message got through properly. But she had very rarely heard him mention dreams, apart from occasional absurd stories to laugh about.

It was the shimmering quality of this dream that made it difficult for her to classify. And hard to forget once she had remembered it. Should she take it as a warning? Should it stop her from doing something she might come to regret? That was easy to believe and it annoyed her. Couldn't she even meet a penfriend without her dreams being full of portents? It was stupid to think that they must have a meaning. Why would all the more or less unconscious thoughts that are ticking over at night be more reliable than those that pass through the mind in its waking state? Of course, there are divided opinions about that. Too many. One could probably analyse that dream into several significant parts. But she didn't care about that.

If Bo came she would be glad to let him in. But before that she had to tidy up the kitchen and living room. The sun was so low that the dust swirled in the sunbeams and all the spills and crumbs could be seen on the table and seats. She didn't think that Bo would be checking for cleanliness, but no-one could fail to notice such disarray. She did not want the house to appear actually dirty.

Just as she was laying a fire in the open fireplace in the living room, the telephone rang. This time she knew who it was.

'Anna,' he said. 'This is Bo Rydeman here. Am I disturbing you or is it all right if I come?'

'That would be absolutely fine. Would you like to have something to eat?'

'Yes please. If you need anything, cheese or bread for example, I can buy a little.'

'Cheese and bread sound fine. I've got everything else. Where are you now?'

'Just before Bålsta.'

'Then it will take a good half an hour for you to get here. Will you be able to find your way easily?'

'I am beginning to be familiar with the road now,' he said and laughed a little.

When she put down the receiver, she sat down to pull herself together. But it really wasn't necessary. The conversation had been so ordinary that one couldn't get palpitations from it. It was entirely prosaic and a bit of an anti-climax in fact. But his voice had sounded nice.

She got up again and stood at the door to the living room. As she looked around she cautiously rubbed her spine with her right hand. To bring in someone she didn't know into her home was almost the same to her as exposing her soul. There were paintings and ornaments which she – and perhaps Håkan – liked but they wouldn't look like much to anybody else. And none of the furniture was so old that it needed to be handled with care. She wasn't at all sure where she would sit with him to drink coffee after the meal. Perhaps it would be awkward. On the other hand it was always easy to sit and talk in front of an open fire. Looking at the flames was relaxing. It remained to be seen how it would turn out.

He would be welcome in her kitchen. It was certainly the heart of the home but at the same time almost a public place. People marched straight into it. The postman, friends, neighbours, guests, plumbers, carpenters... in short, everybody. In the old days the children sat at the kitchen table and swung their legs when they wanted company or had something on their minds. Sometimes their friends sat there as well, often with their own problems and in urgent need of sympathy. In those days she was seldom alone in the kitchen. There wasn't silence around her then.

And now she was expecting a visitor again. Life wasn't over. She felt happy and light-hearted. She must take the cutlets out of the freezer, put the mushrooms in a saucepan and lay the table. There wasn't anything much to do, but the preparations should be got out of the way. She put out the brown ceramic plates and wine glasses, took a step back and examined the result. There was nothing wrong with the kitchen. It was her domain and it was naturally homely. No need to sit rigidly upright and converse carefully at this table. She kept an eye on the clock, tried to empty her head and ward off approaching anxiety. This meeting with Bo was no different from seeing an old friend, she told herself. Just as if old friends tramped in and out of her kitchen every quarter of an hour.

Her thoughts suddenly leaped to Håkan but she got them together again. He didn't have anything to do with it, him and his Dutch witch. This was Anna's own business and needn't concern anyone but her. She went to the window again and looked out although it was much too early for Bo to arrive, particularly as he had to stop and do the shopping on the way. Then she got on with the cooking.

The next time she looked out of the window the postwoman was on the road in her yellow van. 'I hope she contents herself with putting the post in the box by the roadside,' thought Anna, who didn't want to be caught red-handed at the stove.

But no. The postwoman was conscientious. She looked out for the people on her round and she was already in the kitchen entrance after giving a quick knock.

'I didn't know if you could get down to the box now under your own steam,' she said kindly. Then she looked around and eagerly sniffed the air.

'That smells really good. What is it? Garlic, mushrooms or something else?'

'Lamb cutlets with a little thyme.'

The postwoman nodded and glanced at the two plates, the glasses and the rose-pink linen napkins. She didn't say anything but she looked amused. The dimples deepened in her cheeks when she placed the post on the kitchen sofa.

'Goodbye and have a good time,' she called from the entrance.

It was as if she was giving her blessing. Anna wondered if she had made a connection between the two glasses and the wine with the many letters in Bo's sprawling handwriting which she'd delivered here, or if she recognised Håkan's style and saw his name on the back of that white envelope which was now lying on the sofa among *Vi i villa* and a bill from *Tele 2*. Did she mean that Anna was doing the right thing while she had the chance?

She quickly ripped open the envelope, which as usual had the name of the hotel and address printed on the back. She was ready for the worst. That he had already arrived in Sweden, that he was part of the way here and should be fetched, or that the money had run out or some other catastrophe had happened.

'Arriving Arlanda Sunday evening. Want to be picked up, have a cold and am tired.'

Sunday evening. She had three whole days to herself. Three whole days without worry. Then she had to bring home the old runaway, but he seemed to be back to reality at least. Tired and with a cold. This time his journey to paradise had been short. She felt a little sorry for him. The years had caught up with him and that wasn't so funny.

Her lunch might not be that much fun either, she thought with a sudden feeling of uneasiness. Down on the road the yellow post van slowed down as it met a blue car. She put the card into its envelope and laid it down on the writing desk in the study. She would ring Lasse and tell him that his father was on the way home. But there was no hurry for that.

She brushed back the hair at her brow and temples and

drew a breath deep down into her stomach. Then she looked into the oven where the cutlets were quietly bubbling under their cover of mushrooms.

The blue car was already standing on the forecourt and Fabian was receiving it with his usual eagerness. Bo was wearing a Loden coat and dark grey trousers. She couldn't see his face because he'd bent down to greet Fabian. Then he opened the car door and rummaged in the rear seat with his back to her. With an ICA bag in one hand and a flower shop package in the other, he turned around and moved quickly towards the door where she was standing to sneak a look at him through the glass pane. Any reluctance she had felt had gone and was replaced by happy expectation and a strange calm.

He looked kind. He looked very kind as he came towards her carrying presents. And she wasn't exactly overburdened with kindness.

She opened the door wide and stretched out both hands. It was not clear whether it was to welcome him or to receive the flowers and the bag.

In the bright light all the creases around her eyes and the small furrows on her cheeks could clearly be seen. But the thin lines on her upper lip smoothed out when she curved her long thin mouth into a smile. Her white hair shone in the sun and he thought that she looked amazingly healthy. It was almost inconceivable that he continued to have such remarkable luck with women, he thought, feeling elated as he gave her the flowers. She thanked him, smiled, and blushed a little.

'It's so nice of you to come. A sensible person to speak to at last,' she said. 'It's been a bit lonely of late.'

Notes

1   Östermalm is a wealthy residential area of Stockholm with attractive parks and tree-lined streets.

2   The Swedish savings banks' oak tree symbol was invented in the 1920s and registered in 1932 as their trademark.

3   Harriet Löwenhjelm (1887–1918) was a Swedish artist and poet. Her poems were originally a complement to her drawings.

4   Hjalmar Söderberg (1862–1915) was a Swedish novelist, playwright, poet and journalist. His works often deal with melancholy and lovelorn characters. He married Märta Abenius with whom he had three children, but left her for Emelie Voss who was Danish. He managed to arrange for Märta to be admitted to a psychiatric institution which allowed him to divorce her and marry Emelie with whom he had one child.

5   Lydia (Stille) was the lover of Arvid Stjärnblom (see 7 below).

6   Georg Carl von Döbeln (1758–1820) was a Swedish Lieutenant known for his bravery when fighting for Sweden in the Finnish war of 1808–1809.

7   Arvid Stjärnblom was a character in Söderberg's most successful novel – *The Serious Game* (1912).

8   Märta Brehm and Thomas Weber were the principal characters in Söderberg's novel – *Delusions* (1895). Weber fathered Märta's illegitimate child.

9   Harry Martinson (1904–1978) was a Swedish writer who won the Nobel Prize for Literature in 1974. Martinson lost both his parents at a young age and spent his childhood in a series of foster homes. His early experiences are described in two autobiographical novels – *Flowering Nettle* (1935) and *The Way Out* (1936).

10   Tora Dahl (1886–1982) was a Swedish teacher and novelist. She published *Fosterbarn* (Fosterchild) in 1954.

11 Bosse is the diminutive of Bo.
12 Lit. 'You organised and arranged everything and had everyone's interests at heart.'
13 NK (Nordiska Kompaniet) is the name of a luxurious large department store in Stockholm established in 1915.
14 'System' is a state-owned chain of liquor stores in Sweden.
15 ICA is the leading grocery retailer in Sweden.
16 Teskedsgumman (the teaspoon lady or the teaspoon hag) is a fictional character in a series of children's books created by the Norwegian author Alf Prøysen.
17 Jan i Skrolycka is a character in the novel *The Emperor of Portugallia* by Selma Lagerlöf.
18 PI is a national radio channel produced by the Swedish public broadcaster Sverige Radio.
19 A toyshop in Stockholm.
20 The Swedish medicines compendium.
21 Johan Ludwig Runeberg (1804–1877) was a Finnish-Swedish poet, generally considered to be the national poet of Finland. The quote, 'He didn't speak, but his eyes spoke' is from Runeberg's poem *Den enda stunden* ('The Single Moment').
22 'Bojan' is a diminutive of Ingeborg (the name of Bo's mother).
23 The first translation of Winnie the Pooh (by A.A. Milne) into Swedish was actually published in 1930.
24 Hjalmar Gulberg (1898–1961) was a Swedish writer and poet.
25 Lundsberg – a prestigious boarding school.
26 The crawl space is an area of limited height under a floor or roof giving access to wiring and plumbing.
27 Vinterny – a Swedish name meaning 'a new moon in winter'.
28 "Here it was lively, here it was fun, here there were flowers on mother's hat".
29 A significant social event held at the Karlberg Palace in Stockholm.